“I saved the best for last.” Lexi held out a straw cowboy hat. “It’s the tree topper.”

Clint laughed. “I might not know much about decorating, but isn’t it supposed to be a star?”

“Not on a cowboy Christmas tree. The hat is the finishing touch.”

Clint smiled and sidled up next to her, gently taking the ornament from her hand and placing it at the top of the tree.

They stepped back to survey their work. With the colored lights, cowboy ornaments and red bandanas tied here and there, it represented him and all he stood for. Something shifted inside him. Softened his heart.

It was his first Christmas tree, and it suited him perfectly. And it was all because of Lexi.

She turned to hi
work.”

He high-fived he h
this day meant t

“Come on. Pumpkin pie is waiting for us.”

Pumpkin pie, Christmas decorating, laughter and music? He’d better not get used to this; it would be gone all too soon.

Jill Kemerer writes novels with love, humor and faith. Besides spoiling her mini dachshund and keeping up with her busy kids, Jill reads stacks of books, lives for her morning coffee and gushes over fluffy animals. She resides in Ohio with her husband and two children. Jill loves connecting with readers, so please visit her website, jillkemerer.com, or contact her at PO Box 2802, Whitehouse, OH 43571.

Books by Jill Kemerer

Love Inspired

Wyoming Cowboys

The Rancher's Mistletoe Bride

Small-Town Bachelor
Unexpected Family
Her Small-Town Romance
Yuletide Redemption
Hometown Hero's Redemption

The Rancher's Mistletoe Bride

Jill Kemerer

Recycling programs for this product may not exist in your area.

ISBN-13: 978-0-373-62303-7

The Rancher's Mistletoe Bride

This edition published by arrangement with Love Inspired Books.

www.Harlequin.com

Printed in U.S.A.

Do nothing out of selfish ambition or vain conceit. Rather, in humility value others above yourselves, not looking to your own interests but each of you to the interests of the others.

—*Philippians* 2:3–4

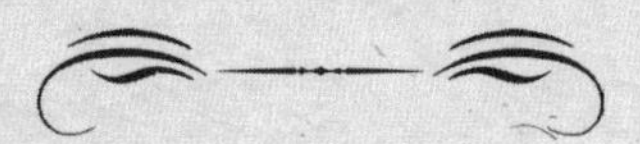

For Rachel Kent. This book wouldn't be here without you. I'm thankful for you every day.

For Pen to Paper, the first writing group I ever joined. Jan and Patricia, your gentleness and knowledge were instrumental to my growth. Thank you.

Chapter One

He hadn't ranched in four years, but the tug of cowboy life always beckoned.

Clint Romine slowed his truck to study the magnificent property splayed before him. Well-maintained fences lined the perimeter and divided areas for rotating stock. Acres of grazing land, fields for hay production, barns, cabins, outbuildings, paddocks—all appeared neat and orderly and only a ten-minute drive from Sweet Dreams, Wyoming. Rock Step Ranch was everything a cattle ranch should be. And more. If Clint's interview went well, he'd be in charge of this entire outfit.

Unease slithered down his neck. Was he fit to manage it?

His mistake haunted him. A slip in his judgment. The death of a dream. But owning a ranch wasn't the same as being hired to manage one. Four years ago, he'd had everything to lose. And now? There was nothing left for him to lose. He'd already lost it all.

Clint drove into a gravel lot near the barn and paddocks, cut the engine, and stepped out. Mountains stood proudly in the distance, and the wind held the bite of early November. Cowboys shouted from the cutting pen.

Looked like they were weaning calves. He longed to slap on his chaps and join them.

After watching for a few minutes, he checked the time and forced himself to stride toward the main house. A two-story log home with a covered porch, a pair of rocking chairs and a faded mat greeted him. Before he knocked, he paused to pray.

Lord, I've made mistakes. I don't deserve my own land. But if You'll give me the opportunity to manage this operation, I'll try not to let You or the ranch down.

Clint stretched himself to his full height and rapped twice on the door. It opened almost immediately, and he stared into light brown eyes the color of the pronghorns he often saw bounding across the land.

Alexandra Harrington had grown into a beautiful woman.

He wasn't in her league—had never been in her league. When he'd found out she was the one hiring, he'd been concerned about working for his former classmate. Attraction complicated the employer/employee relationship. When he'd worked on LFR Ranch, a cowboy had been fired for flirting with the owner's daughter. But now that he'd seen Alexandra, his fears disappeared. A smart, successful, stunning woman like her was out of reach for a working guy like him. Not that he needed to worry about it. Rumor had it you had to spend time with a woman, get to know her, to have a shot at dating her. He had no intention of spending time with her, let alone dating her.

"Thanks for coming, Clint." She ushered him inside, and once he'd taken off his outerwear, he followed her down a hallway to a large living room with views of the river. The hardwood floors were in bad shape. Scratched. Faded. Three rocks were missing from the stone fireplace climbing the wall to the ceiling. From somewhere nearby, the drip, drip of a faucet fought to override the sound of a ripped screen flapping against a window. Even the air had the stale tang of neglect.

Strange that the outbuildings, fences and property were in top-notch order, but this house had been allowed to fall apart.

He turned his attention to the woman he recognized from high school. Still slim in dark jeans and an oversize white sweater. Long, dark brown waves spilled over her shoulders. Her pale face held high cheekbones, full eyebrows and thin pink lips. But Alexandra wore sad the way he wore regret—it permeated her, surrounded her—and he had the strongest urge to take it from her. Which was a laugh, since he had no idea how. He'd never been around many women and probably never would be.

He *did* know what it was like to suddenly have no family, though. Her father had died three weeks ago. She had every right to be sad.

She took a seat on an old tan couch, motioning for him to sit opposite her, and he obliged, his cowboy hat in his hands.

"Dottie Lavert mentioned you might be interested in managing the ranch for me." Her words were quiet but firm. "As you know, Daddy died unexpectedly, and I need someone here sooner rather than later."

He nodded, not knowing what to think of the way she was fingering the bottom edge of her sweater. Was she nervous? No. This was Alexandra Harrington. Vice president of their senior class, organizer of proms and dances and who knew what else.

"I remember you from high school," she said. "You worked on a ranch then, too, didn't you?"

"Yes." He was surprised she remembered him at all. His one goal in high school had been to be as invisible as possible. As a teen, he'd poured all his energy into keeping his spot at Yearling Group Home for teen boys. The Laverts had been hired to run the group foster home. Back then, Big Bob Lavert kept the boys in line while his wife, Dottie, cooked their meals, made sure they did their homework and accompanied them to church. Too bad Yearling had shut down several years ago. It had helped a lot of kids like him who had nowhere else to go.

"From your résumé, I see you've been working for the oil company." She smiled, her expression open, expectant. "And before that you worked on LFR Ranch."

"Yes, ma'am."

"Call me Lexi."

Lexi? He couldn't call her Lexi. Couldn't even think of her as Lexi. Too familiar, too accessible. *Alexandra* had the right amount of remoteness for his liking.

"I learned about calving, grazing, hay production, keeping the books and maintaining the property from my years at LFR." He paused, unsure how much more to tell her. If he confessed how he'd left LFR and then been duped out of his own tiny piece of Wyoming, she'd boot him right out the door. And if he admitted he'd spent four years avoiding working on a ranch because it had hurt too much to be surrounded by what he'd lost, she'd think he was crazy. "I've been working for the oil company for four years now."

She picked up the top paper from a stack on the end table next to her. "Yes, I see you were promoted three times in as many years. Impressive."

Impressive? Him? If she only knew… He hoped she didn't ask about the six months between LFR Ranch and the oil company. If asked outright, he wouldn't lie to her. And he didn't want to return to his mind-numbing job.

"I need someone I can depend on to do all the things my father did. I own a wedding planning company in Denver. I've already told my employees I'll be living in Wyoming at least until Christmas. To put it simply, my business takes all of my time. If running my company from here proves too difficult, I'll have to move back to Colorado. In that case, I'd come to the ranch once a month or so. I need someone here who is self-motivated. Someone who can delegate work to the ranch hands. Someone I can trust."

Could she trust him? Did he trust himself?

She continued. "The next question might seem forward, but I have to know. Do you drink?"

"No."

She narrowed her eyes, her lips pursing, clearly unconvinced.

"I've seen what it does to people and have no desire to try it." He held her gaze. "I like to be in complete control of my faculties. At all times. I'll take a drug test if you'd like."

"I'll take your word for it." She massaged the back of her neck. She looked tired. More than tired. Exhausted. "You're not the first person to be considered for this position. I hired a man last week who had a problem with the hard stuff. What a disaster he turned out to be. Daddy's right-hand man, Jerry Cornell—you'll meet him in a little while—found him at noon on Saturday still lit out of his mind, sitting in the river in his drawers when he should have been working. When I called him into the office, he had the nerve to tell me not to worry my 'purdy' little head about it. Needless to say, I had to let him go." She got to her feet and started pacing. "He's fortunate he didn't get hypothermia."

Clint strangled the hat between his hands. He'd worked with plenty of cowboys who drank too much. The fact one of them would disrespect her made him want to rope the jerk up.

She spun to face him, chin high. "This is my home. The only thing left of my childhood and my parents. I have ranch hands and their families depending on me for their income. If keeping this operation profitable and in tip-top shape isn't your number-one priority, you will not work here. It's that simple. And, in case I didn't make it clear, I have the final say in all ranch decisions."

"Yes, ma'am." He could keep a ranch in tip-top shape. But profitable? He'd made a bad financial choice years ago. What if he made one again?

She sighed then, her body sagging as if someone had let the air out of her. "I'll take you out to meet Jerry. He'll show you around and feed you lunch. When you're done, come back up here and we'll talk."

Good. She was a take-charge woman unafraid to be his boss. The firmer the line between employee and employer, the better. As long as he made wise decisions concerning the cattle, he could spend his days doing what he loved best—living the cowboy life.

Working for the prettiest girl he'd ever laid eyes on.

Living the *single* cowboy life.

Pretty or not, no woman would want a man who'd been stupid enough to get swindled out of the one thing he'd ever wanted—a ranch of his own.

"Well, Jerry, what do you think?" Lexi sat on a stool in the ranch manager's office adjoining the stables. The room smelled of dirt, large animals and burned coffee. Everywhere she looked, she found clutter of the male kind. Ropes, broken bridles, spray cans full of who knew what, stained papers and tools. Her office in Denver was painted the pale pink of a rose petal and smelled of magnolias. She missed it.

Which brought her back to the three-week-old question…why was she still here? After the funeral, she'd packed her suitcase with every intention of driving back to her life in Denver. She hadn't made it off the property before turning around, filled with the sensation she was deserting the place, the same way she'd deserted her father to focus on expanding her company.

Where did she belong? Here with her memories or back in the city with Weddings by Alexandra?

"Clint's a good 'un, Miss Lexi." The wire-thin man scratched his chin and scanned Clint's résumé. "His former bosses paint him as a fine man."

She thought as much, too, but it was reassuring to hear it from Jerry. She tapped a pen against her chin. "Any reason you can think of why I shouldn't hire him?"

"Nope." He rolled the paper and smacked it on the plywood counter.

Taking it from Jerry, she uncurled it. Perused it once more. "What about the gap between jobs? It was four years ago, but…"

Jerry shook his head. "A lot of cowboys have periods they can't account for."

"Really? Why?"

"Ah…well…these are lonely parts up here in this blessed country. You know those wild horses that run wild through the north property now and again?"

"Yes."

"Some cowboys are like those horses. They don't like to be fenced in. Something snaps, and they leave. Could be due to a lady. Could be a sense they need to move on."

Clint was the wild horse in this scenario, but he seemed quiet, steady. She bit her tongue. She'd been listening to Jerry's parables her entire life, and they tended to meander.

"Now some of the boys take their savings and go off and live awhile. Figure things out. Get close to the land and their maker…"

It made sense. Everyone needed time to figure life out now and then. Wasn't that what she herself was doing?

"…but the restlessness clears up, and they settle down right fine."

She hopped off the stool. "Okay, Jerry, I'll take your word for it. Send him up to the house when Logan brings him back."

"Will do." He gave her a nod. "Oh, and Miss Lexi?"

"Yes?"

"The Florida fella called again. Wants to know if he can count on us for hay next winter."

Lexi tucked her hair behind her ear. One of her father's pet projects had been to start growing high-quality hay to sell to horse farms and other large-animal breeders across the nation. He'd built the new storage barn in the spring and begun negotiations with various buyers. But the drought conditions coupled with low calf prices last year prevented him from purchasing the necessary equipment to produce the square bales. Putting up high-quality hay had been postponed until next summer.

"I don't know the answer. It will depend on the price we get for this year's calves."

"I'll call him and tell him we'll know more in a few months."

"Thanks, Jerry." She left the office, savoring the fresh air as she headed back to her house. Between the ranch and her business, there seemed to be an endless list of problems. For weeks, Lexi's assistant, Jolene Day, had been texting her every three minutes with an urgent crisis. Two clients had called earlier with major changes to their weddings, and the invitations Lexi had ordered two months ago were still on back order.

And then there was the ranch. Daddy had been the spine of this operation, and without him? If she didn't find a take-charge manager, she would have to sell Rock Step Ranch. She couldn't manage both, and she'd rather have someone else own it than let Daddy's legacy fade to ruins.

Just thinking about selling made her nauseous. This was her home. Her memories.

As she reached the path leading to her house, a gust of wind blew her scarf across her face, and she swept it back. Clint seemed to be the perfect candidate for manager, but if she were brutally honest with herself, he presented a new dilemma. One he couldn't help.

He was gorgeous.

And tall. Solid muscle. Quiet.

The gorgeous part was the problem.

She'd never expected to be attracted to him. She barely remembered him from high school. In fact, she couldn't recall having a single conversation with him back then. How had she overlooked him? He had thick, dark hair begging to be touched, and his midnight blue eyes seemed to notice everything. He was as fine a physical specimen as she'd ever seen.

A rugged, handsome cowboy.

Thankfully, he was all wrong for her. The strong, silent types were perfect for managing a ranch, but as far as dating? Not likely to sweep her off her feet any time soon.

She opened the front door and took off her coat and boots before heading to the living room and sitting on the couch. Her cell phone showed missed calls and texts, but she only checked the one from Jerry. Clint was on his way.

Even if she hadn't been overwhelmed trying to make double the business decisions as usual, she couldn't imagine dating anyone at this time and certainly not Clint. She wanted romance with a capital *R*, and after Doug, she'd decided under no circumstances was she settling for ho-hum. She wanted breathless kisses. Heart-pounding anticipation. A man who loved her enough to make a grand gesture or two. Someone who valued marriage and wanted kids.

She wanted more than any guy had offered her so far, and Clint, for all his curling eyelashes and silky, touchable hair, seemed too reserved to be that guy.

Besides, she *had* to hire him. She was out of options. She'd interviewed five men for the job, hired one, fired one. With the drought and extra expenses from the new barn, the ranch needed someone with experience who understood how to manage its resources wisely. And after losing Daddy, she couldn't bear to lose her home, too.

A knock on the door startled her. She opened it, once more struck by Clint's blue eyes. She waved for him to follow her into the living room.

"Well, what did you think?"

He perched on the edge of the chair, hat in hand. "It's a

fine operation. Jerry's done a good job running it since… well…" His eyebrows drew together, and he cleared his throat.

"Yes." She clasped her hands tightly. Thinking about Daddy being gone formed an instant lump in her throat, one she'd gotten adept at ignoring. Somehow she needed to find a way to get over the pain of losing him that had taken up permanent residence in her heart. "Jerry's been a blessing. For many years."

"Why don't you have him manage it?" The question was simple, open, pure curiosity.

"He doesn't want to. His wife's been asking him to slow down. He's getting older. Said I needed a long-term solution. And Logan isn't interested, either. He's the most experienced full-time ranch hand, but he only plans on staying here a year or two more. He and his wife want to move back to Casper after they save enough money to buy a house."

Clint nodded, a lock of hair dipping across his forehead. She forced her attention to her raggedy fingernails. Flipping through the papers she'd left on the end table earlier, she found the list she'd typed.

"Jerry and I discussed it, and we think you're right for the position." After naming his salary and benefits, she went over his duties and wrapped it up with living arrangements. "We have a few empty cabins, a two-bedroom guest house and a three-bedroom manager's house. Logan lives in the manager's house with his wife, Sarah, and their children. She's the ranch cook. If you'd like, I'll ask them to move, but…"

"No." He shook his head. "One of the cabins will be fine."

"Does this mean you'll take the job?"

"I'll take it." His eyes glinted, reminding her of a wild storm on the prairie, all lightning flashes and black clouds rolling in the distance. Spectacular. Exciting.

Maybe Jerry was onto something with the whole wild horse analogy. And maybe Clint wasn't as reserved as she'd originally thought.

"When can you start?" she asked.

"When do you need me?"

"Yesterday." She sighed, waving her hand. "Sorry, it's just been hard on the crew. They've all had to step up and take on way too much responsibility here for weeks now. I know you need to give your employer notice and—"

"I'll move in this weekend and start Monday."

Just like that? She wanted to raise her fist and yell, "Yippee!" but she said a silent prayer of thanks instead. "Perfect. As for the living arrangements, I appreciate you allowing Logan and Sarah to stay in the larger house, but I insist you take the two-bedroom guest cabin. You're in a position of authority here, and your lodging should reflect it."

He nodded.

"Do you have any questions?" she asked. "Any concerns?"

"No, ma'am."

"Clint, we graduated high school together. *Ma'am* makes me feel like I'm a hundred and fifty years old. Call me Lexi."

"I don't know if I feel right doing that."

"Why not?"

"Well, if you're going to be my boss, I think it should be more formal."

"I will be your boss, but we're going to have to be comfortable enough with each other that you can come to me with any problems. We'll be meeting weekly on Thursday mornings to discuss the ranch. I might not be involved in the daily operations, but I am very invested in its future."

"I'm glad to hear that. This is your ranch. You should be invested."

"Exactly. Jerry has paperwork for you to fill out. I'll meet you down there in half an hour to show you to your new home." She held out her hand. "Thanks, Clint, for coming today. Welcome aboard."

The warm strength in his callused hand assured her she'd chosen wisely. He dipped his head and left. As soon as the front door clicked shut, she went to the kitchen to make a cup of tea. Her hand trembled as she filled the cup. She kept forgetting to eat. Maybe a piece of toast to go with the tea…

How had her life changed so drastically? One minute she was on top of the world, succeeding at her dream job. The next, plunged into the abyss of her father's death.

Six months. That's how long it had been since she'd visited Daddy. He'd appeared to be in fine health in May. They'd ridden on horseback around the ranch the way they always did. She'd had no idea he had cancer.

Had he known?

Of course not.

If he had known, he would have told her. She would have come back, gone to the doctor with him, made sure he got chemotherapy and radiation and anything that would have saved him. But they hadn't known. And now it was too late.

Why didn't I make more of an effort to come home this summer? He must have been sick. Must have had some *symptoms. And I wasn't here to notice.*

Her throat tightened the way it had repeatedly since she'd gotten the call from Jerry saying her father had died.

When she'd told Clint this ranch was the only thing left of her parents and her childhood, she'd meant it. And she wasn't about to lose it, too.

As Lexi gave him the tour of the two-bedroom log cabin, Clint mentally tallied a to-do list. It was dusty, but the open area with the kitchen, dining and living room was larger than his current apartment's, and the master bedroom had a nice view of the mountains. He planned to take his coffee first thing each day on the covered porch. Frankly, it was the nicest place he'd lived in and, even unfurnished, it felt like home.

Home. A sense of foreboding killed his good mood. Had he ever belonged anywhere? If he started identifying this place as home, he'd lose it, the way he'd been torn from every other place where he'd felt comfortable.

He needed to remain detached.

At least the main house was up the lane far enough for him to maintain a necessary distance from his boss. Other than weekly meetings, he saw no reason why they would need to see each other.

"The river's great for fishing, and feel free to use the ATVs anytime. If you need help moving in, just holler. I'm sure one of the ranch hands would be happy to lend a hand."

"Yes, ma'a—" He caught himself. "Thank you, Miss Lexi."

She leaned against the kitchen counter and glared. "Clint, Jerry, who is seventy-five years old, calls me Miss Lexi. It's Lexi. Just Lexi."

He itched to smile, but she looked paler, more tired than she had earlier. He studied her more closely.

Thin. Too thin. Dark smudges under her eyes. Cheekbones jutting out. Her clothes hung on her. Was she eating enough? Or at all?

She had the look of someone who'd had to be strong for too long. It reminded him of moving into his first foster home after his grandfather died when Clint was six. Even though Grandpa had been mean as a rattler, when the man passed, Clint knew deep inside he was all alone in the world and his life would never be the same. Did Lexi feel alone, too? He wanted to tuck her under a blanket on the couch. Protect her.

He shook his head. Him protecting her? What a laugh. She didn't need someone like him.

She stepped forward and wobbled.

"Have you eaten lately?" He moved closer, ready to catch her if she fainted.

"What?" She blinked, shaking her head, and swayed. He reached for her, steadied her.

"Come on, I'll take you back. You need some food."

"I'm fine." Her protest sounded weak. "I had some toast a little bit ago."

"It's five thirty. You need a meal." He kept a loose hold on her arm and led her to the door. The wind had picked up, and the temperature had dropped. "Zip up. You don't want to catch cold."

To his relief, she didn't argue. She zipped her coat and fell in beside him. When they reached the house, he followed her inside. A napkin with a half-eaten piece of toast lay on the end table. Probably the only food she'd eaten today.

"Sit on the couch, and I'll make you something to eat."

"I couldn't ask you—"

"I'm not driving back to Cheyenne on an empty stomach. I'll make some supper and get out of here."

She sat on the couch, looking lost. "Okay."

He opened her fridge and pantry. Chicken broth, noodles, frozen carrots. "Are you saving the chicken in the freezer for anything?"

"There's chicken in the freezer?"

He chuckled under his breath. "I'm using it."

After opening cupboards and drawers, he had a good idea of where everything was stored. He chopped an onion, defrosted and diced the chicken, and heated oil in a frying pan. He filled a large pot with the chicken stock and set it on the stove to boil.

Lexi crept up and sat on one of the bar stools opposite him. "What are you making?"

"Chicken noodle soup."

"Really, you can cook?"

He nodded, suddenly uncomfortable. He shouldn't be here, in her house, going through her kitchen. It was too intimate.

She wiped her fingers across her forehead. "I never really learned." Her cell phone rang. "Excuse me." She hurried to stand by the patio door as she answered the phone.

After stirring the chicken frying in the pan, he tracked her moves. Voice bright and confident, hand reaching for the pen and paper on the coffee table. Phone tucked between her ear and shoulder as she scribbled something. When the call ended, she seemed to deflate, and he quickly turned away.

"I forgot to mention I'll be out of town next Thursday through Sunday. It's the final wedding I'm in charge of for the year. My other planners are organizing the rest."

"Okay." He slid the cooked chicken into the boiling pot along with the noodles, onions and carrots. A pinch of salt and pepper, and he dialed the burner down to simmer for a while. "If you don't cook, what do you do for meals?"

"Well, in Denver, I order a lot of takeout. I'm usually working late, anyhow."

"But you're here. And there's no takeout."

"I manage."

Not very well, from the looks of it. He doubted she'd eaten more than a bowl of cereal all week. "Why don't you eat with the rest of the crew?"

She grimaced, shaking her head vehemently. "I wouldn't feel comfortable, and neither would they."

She had a point there. "You mentioned a cook—Sarah, right? She would probably fix you a plate."

Lexi shrugged, a wistful expression in her eyes. "I'm sure you're right."

He could tell she had no intention of asking Sarah for a meal. He'd stop over at the manager's house soon and have a quick chat with Logan and his wife. One of the hands could pick up a meal from them to drop off at the main house each night. Whether Lexi ate it or not wasn't his concern.

Her phone rang again. She smiled an apology and answered it, walking away. He couldn't imagine a job with constant phone calls. He stirred the soup, decided it was ready, and ladled out a bowl for her. She was sitting in a chair, saying something about bouquets and cost overages. He'd done his duty. Made her food. She wouldn't even notice if he left without eating. Sharing a meal with her seemed a little too cozy at this point.

But as he sneaked out to his truck, his mind kept returning to her and the bowl of soup he'd left. He didn't want her fainting. Didn't like that her clothes were hanging from her.

She's not my problem.

He'd been hired to manage the ranch, not the ranch owner. Sure, she was alone and grieving and not taking proper care of herself, but fixing it wasn't within his realm.

As he drove past the paddocks, he barely noticed the property that had so mesmerized him earlier. He'd better get his focus back on the cattle and the land where it belonged. He'd finally gotten the nerve to try working on a ranch again. He couldn't make another mistake and ruin this, too.

Chapter Two

Visions of weddings and twinkle lights and Clint filled Lexi's head. Well, not all three together. She sprayed glass cleaner on the new desk she'd installed in the front den. Clint was only on her mind because he was on his way over for their first official ranch meeting. She hoped it wouldn't be awkward. The weddings and twinkle lights were remnants from the weekend, when she'd organized her final wedding of the year.

Two weeks had passed since she'd hired Clint, and she hadn't seen him much, except in passing. They'd nod and exchange pleasantries before going their separate ways. Strictly business.

Strictly business was good. She could pour her energy into weddings, where it belonged. Except she kept thinking back to the night she'd hired him. He'd cooked her soup. Soup! And it had been the best chicken noodle soup she'd ever tasted. She'd indulged in two bowls that night. She'd slept well, too, which was saying something, considering her sleep had been spotty and elusive for a long time.

After wiping the desk clean, she straightened the

shelves and displayed the latest bridal magazines she'd brought back with her from Denver. She moved the floor lamp to the corner and studied it before picking it up once more.

"Can I help you with that?" Clint stood in the doorway. He wore a plaid navy-and-white Western shirt with jeans and boots, and a file was tucked under his arm.

"No, just finishing up." She plastered on her brightest smile. "Come in. Sit down. Would you like something to drink?"

"No, thanks."

"Well, have a seat." She sat in the swivel chair behind the desk and fired up her laptop. "How is your house? Are you settling in okay?"

"It's fine."

Didn't exactly answer her question, but she wasn't surprised. Something told her their weekly meetings weren't going to be as conversational as the ones she led in Denver. She was used to chatting about the latest trends in weddings in her chic conference room with her team of creative professionals. Talking about the ranch with Clint would most likely be brief and to the point.

Clint was currently eyeing her new office. She almost laughed at the frightened look on his face when his gaze landed on her vision board. Swatches of silks, photos of various flowers and motivational quotes in gold calligraphy adorned it.

She took pity on him and clicked through to the checklist she'd created. "Before we get started, I think you should know I've never been involved in ranch operations. Growing up, I helped Daddy move cattle, of course, but…well, you know more about this than I do." She scanned the notes she'd typed after asking Jerry what to expect on the ranch each month. "Let's see… I'm assuming the calves have all been weaned?"

"Yes, they were actually weaned by the time I moved in. We're keeping a close eye on them. Getting ready to sell. I looked over your winter feed program. We'll continue your father's plan this year."

"As opposed to what plan?" She enjoyed watching him as he talked. Cattle seemed to loosen his tongue; animation lit his face.

"The calf sale date is on the books for the second week in December." He brought his hand to the back of his neck. "But prices will rise after the new year, and if we spent the money to feed the calves longer, they'd weigh more, and we'd get a bigger return on investment."

The words *bigger return on investment* were precisely what she loved to hear. "Do you have numbers?"

He opened his folder and handed her a sheet of paper. A spreadsheet held the number of cattle, the amount of feed needed through the winter and the estimated calf sale price for every month until March.

"But what about the drought? Will we have enough hay stored to feed them along with the rest of the cattle?"

"We would have to supplement with outside feed." He sounded gruff.

"Which, I'm assuming, would be expensive." She wasn't sure how to read him, so she studied the spreadsheet more carefully. "What you're suggesting—do you think it would be smarter to wait a few months to sell the calves?"

He didn't make eye contact. "I think you should do what's best for the ranch."

"Which is?"

"There are pros and cons to both."

Lexi tapped the desktop with her fingernails. He didn't seem the wishy-washy type, so why was he dithering? Maybe he'd taken her declaration about having the final say in all decisions personally.

Or maybe he wasn't the take-charge guy she needed for the ranch after all.

Jerry had assured her they had enough hay stored to feed the cattle this winter. But feeding additional calves? Not likely.

"We'll stay on Daddy's plan this year." Tipping her chin up, she asked, "What else do I need to know?"

He shifted his jaw before filling her in on the state of the fences, the repairs he and the hands were working on, and other winter preparations.

"Are you having any trouble with the employees?" She folded her hands and leaned forward across the desk.

"I'm keeping an eye on Jake."

"Jake?" She twisted her lips, trying to remember a Jake.

"The kid you recently hired. He's part-time."

"Has he done something?"

Clint shrugged. "A gut instinct. I have a zero-tolerance policy for breaking the rules."

"No three strikes you're out?" she teased.

"No." He didn't crack a smile.

Hmm… Hard to tell if he had a sense of humor hiding under all his toughness. She tried to picture a kid named Jake again. She made a point to interact with all the employees of Weddings by Alexandra, and she didn't even know all the people working on her land. It was time to change that.

"Where will you be this afternoon?"

"South pasture. Riding the fence line."

"I'll join you. It's been a while since I've ridden the property. You can introduce me to the crew when we saddle up."

He opened his mouth as if to protest, then nodded. "Meet me at the stables after dinner."

She'd lived in Denver long enough to think of the midday meal as lunch, but around here, she'd better get used to thinking of it as dinner again. She rose to see him out. On his way past the living room, Clint stopped and looked around. The muscle in his cheek flickered.

"Is something wrong?"

"No." Then he tipped his hat to her and left.

What was the tension in him all about?

Was he mad she'd decided to stick with her father's plan?

Her phone showed six missed calls and eight texts. She didn't have time to worry about his feelings. Back in her office, she opened her email account to twenty-six fresh messages. Looking over her schedule, she exhaled in relief. The video conference call wasn't until tomorrow. She'd squish everything in to take an hour or two off this afternoon. She hadn't ridden Nugget, her favorite horse, since May.

A vision of her and Daddy riding together filled her mind, and she willed away the knot in her throat. Had he been thinner the last time she saw him? Shouldn't there have been warning signs cancer was killing his body?

How many times had she thought she should call and check up on him? But she'd put it off. Too busy replying to texts and placing orders and calling clients.

And now it was too late.

She squeezed her eyes shut.

Lord, I don't know how to get through this. Every time I think of Daddy, I can't breathe.

She curled her fingers into her palms. Her father hadn't raised a coward. He'd always told her two things: "Keep your word good" and "Don't forget to close the gate."

She had a feeling she'd offended Clint earlier, and she couldn't afford to lose him, not when he'd taken the weight of worrying about the ranch off her back. She hoped riding the land where she'd spent so many hours with her father wouldn't be too difficult and the tears she'd suppressed for weeks stayed down under, where they belonged.

Clint ignored the harsh wind on his face and admired Nugget, the fifteen-hand palomino Lexi rode. A beauty of a horse. And the woman riding it? Could have been born in the saddle.

Lexi was intriguing. Sophisticated, yet completely at ease with all the ranch employees she'd shaken hands with before they'd ridden out. A shrewd businesswoman, yet utterly feminine. Sitting in her office earlier had felt like sitting in the center of a wedding bouquet. He'd never felt so out of place in his life. He preferred his ranch office with tools, rope, rags and the smells of earth and cattle.

Once again, the state of her house picked at his conscience. He'd noticed it all again when he'd left their meeting. The dripping faucet. The torn screen. The worn, neglected air of the place. The missing stones from the fireplace.

The fireplace flue probably hadn't been cleaned out

in years. What if she wanted to build a fire? It could be dangerous.

Not my problem. I'm her employee. And my place on this ranch will be secure as long as I keep my mouth shut and the operation running smoothly.

The longer he worked on the ranch, the more impressed he became. He hadn't felt this alive in a long time. But as remarkable as the ranch was, its income and expenses were precarious this year.

Jerry had told him all about RJ Harrington's plans to produce and store hay to sell throughout the country, but Clint didn't see how they could afford to buy the farm equipment this winter.

The prices of cattle lately were low. Too low.

Should he have urged her to wait to sell the calves? When Lexi had asked his opinion earlier, he'd blanked. The decision had felt as important as pressing the button to launch a nuclear bomb. He'd mentally gone back to the day when he'd lost his land, the day he'd stopped trusting himself. And instead of telling her what he really thought, he'd backed down.

Lexi deserved better than that.

He glanced at her again. She didn't trust him. He was used to it. As far as he could remember, no one had ever trusted him until they'd gotten to know him, and most never did. His grandfather had called him a worthless brat on a daily basis. Foster parents watched him with the eyes of a red-tailed hawk. Teachers referred to him as *that Romine kid.* Employers gave him the lowliest jobs before giving him the benefit of the doubt.

Trust had to be earned.

And Lexi was right not to trust him. He hadn't told her about losing his land. But if he had, would she have hired him? Doubtful. And anyhow, he was doing everything in his power to manage Rock Step Ranch wisely.

They approached the fence line.

"I haven't been to this pasture in a few years." Her voice was muffled, and he strained to hear her. She faced him then, her light brown eyes wide and watery. Was the wind ripping the moisture from them, or was she about to cry?

He stilled. This was his boss, and he didn't have much experience around tears.

She turned Nugget to the east. Ridges and gullies of windblown grass and sage surrounded them.

"Daddy and I used to ride out to check fences before I got so caught up in high school activities. I must have been eleven or twelve when we came out here on a day like this. Cold. But it hadn't snowed yet. I'd missed a sleepover party at my friend's house, so I was sulking. But coming out here with Daddy made my troubles disappear."

Clint hung on every word. He almost wanted to raise his hand, to tell her to stop, to not say anything more, because sharing memories, no matter how small, would bind them. Even if he didn't reply, he'd get more invested in Lexi as a person than he already was.

And he needed her to be Lexi, the nice lady he worked for, not Lexi, the woman he could care about.

She swept her arm across the land. "He noticed everything. An elk off in the distance, the remains of a snake near the fence where a hawk had made its meal. I remember thinking there was nothing better in the world than being out here with him. Daddy was smarter and kinder than anyone I knew. And we could just be quiet, be ourselves. You know what I mean?"

Clint did. It was how he felt about his best friends, three other foster kids from his days at Yearling Group Home. When he got together with Marshall, Wade and Nash, he didn't have to force a conversation. He could just be himself.

She lifted her face to the sky. "Every time we'd end a ride, I'd give him the biggest hug and say, 'I love you, Daddy.' And he would always tug on my braid or ponytail and reply, 'You, too, kiddo.'"

Clint's heart was doing funny things. He'd never experienced what she described, but it moved him just the same.

"I would do about anything to be able to give him another hug and say those words again," she said softly.

Clint moved his horse closer to her and reached over to take her hand. Her suede gloves didn't dull the connection, and she stared at him, a tear dropping from her eye. Without thinking, he swung off his horse and held his hands out to help her down. When she'd dismounted, he drew her close, sliding a clean handkerchief out of his pocket to give her. Her slender frame shook with tears, but she didn't wind her arms around him. She simply let him pat her back and murmur comfort.

How long they stood like that, Clint had no idea—could have been a minute or an hour—but at some point, Lexi wiped her eyes free of tears and blew her nose into the handkerchief.

"Sorry, I don't know what came over me. I have to get back." She set her foot in the stirrup and swung her leg over the saddle. "I won't keep you. You stay and check the fence."

He watched her urge Nugget into motion. Off to spend the rest of the day answering calls and doing whatever wedding planners did. And from what he could tell, she'd been doing it nonstop since she'd hired him. Which left no time for grieving…

It hit him then. No wonder she was as thin as a piece of licorice. She hadn't grieved her father's death.

There was no one here to look after her. No clients to meet with. No friends to force her to eat lunch. No father to ensure she lived in a safe, well-maintained house.

Nobody but him.

He slapped his thigh and mounted his horse. Miles of checking fence wouldn't be enough to pretend something hadn't shifted inside where Lexi Harrington was concerned, and he didn't like it. Not one bit.

Lexi pulled her favorite velvety blanket up to her chin and pressed the mute button on the remote. Ever since leaving Clint in the pasture earlier, she'd been unable to work. Tears kept erupting.

Because everything here, in this house and on the ranch, reminded her of her father.

Things she hadn't noticed for weeks—his favorite coffee mug, the faded hand towel with an embroidered cowboy boot she'd bought him for his birthday—unleashed her memories. Two hours ago she'd walked past the master bedroom's closed door, the one she hadn't opened since finding out he'd died, and her feet had backtracked until she stood face-to-face with the pine door. Without thought, she'd fallen to her knees, sobbing in front of it.

It was at that point she'd given up on getting anything done. She'd changed into sweatpants, brewed a pot of tea and flipped through the channels until she found one playing original romantic Christmas movies. They always made her feel better.

Not today, though.

Thanksgiving was a week away. She would be celebrating the holidays alone. Oh, she could drive to Denver, join friends with their families, but she wouldn't. Her heart couldn't take being surrounded by happy people, people who would want to cheer her up. She was in no state to fake pleasantries while choking on tears as she ate their turkey dinner.

And she couldn't believe she'd broken down in front of Clint. The man probably thought she'd lost her mind. Maybe she *had* lost her mind. What had possessed her to start telling him those personal things?

Unacceptable on her part. She wasn't paying Clint to be her therapist. The poor guy. Probably worried she was having a nervous breakdown. She'd apologize. Assure him it wouldn't happen again.

Her phone rang.

Clint.

Her palms grew moist. Oh, why had she dissolved into a weepy mess in front of him?

"Hi." His deep voice calmed her nerves. "One of the herding dogs is missing. Banjo, the older one. I didn't want to bother you, but I'm concerned and… Have you seen him?"

Banjo, Daddy's favorite border collie? "No, I haven't. Have you tried the barns?"

"Yeah, I'll keep looking." He sounded like he was going to hang up.

"Wait!" She threw off the blanket, tired of being alone. "I'll come with you."

"It's not necessary. I know you're busy—"

"I'm coming."

"Lexi," he said in his low, soothing tone. It was the

first time she'd heard him use her name, and it did something funny to her pulse. "I don't want to upset you."

"Look, I know I was overly emotional earlier, but that's not me. I don't cry all the time."

"No, that's not what I mean." He sighed. "Dogs hide when they're sick or when it's their time."

His words hit her in the gut. It was true. Dogs were social animals, but when it was their time, they slunk away to die by themselves.

Not Banjo. Not on top of everything else.

"I can handle it, Clint." She couldn't handle it, but being the boss meant dealing with tough situations.

Three minutes later, she wrapped her scarf more tightly around her neck and shivered as Clint handed her a flashlight. Dusk had fallen, and shadows lurked.

"I've checked the stables, the barns, all the obvious places." Clint strode tall and confident toward the cabins. He had the air of a man in command, and right now, she needed someone else to be in charge. "Unless you can think of someplace the dog would have gone… I figure he might have followed one of the cowboys home."

"It's worth a shot." She kept pace with him. "When did you last see him?"

"He trailed in behind Logan and Mike when they returned from checking calves, but he didn't come in with the other dogs at feeding time."

Nothing but the sound of the wind and their feet against the hard dirt met her ears. The fact Banjo hadn't eaten was a bad sign. Where would the dog go if not with the other dogs in the barn? Coyotes were common in these parts. He couldn't have been attacked, could he? Banjo knew better than to tangle with one of them.

They rounded the bend where windows in three of the cabins glowed.

"Why don't you ask Logan and Sarah if they've seen him while I ask the other guys?"

She nodded. After knocking on the door, she rubbed her hands together. Felt like snow was on its way.

"Lexi, what a nice surprise!" Sarah, a pretty blonde in her late twenties, beckoned her to enter, but Lexi stayed on the porch.

"I don't mean to bother you, but Banjo's missing. Have you seen him around tonight?"

The smile slid off Sarah's face. "No, I haven't, and I've always been fond of that dog. Did you check all the barns? He might be trying to stay warm."

"Clint checked already, but we'll try again." Lexi turned to leave. "Oh, and thanks for supper every night, Sarah. You don't have to do that."

"Well, we're all sorry about RJ's passing. He was a good man. Treated us like family. Anything you need, just ask."

"Thank you." Lexi's throat tightened as she turned away. *Not again.* What was it with today? If she cried one more time, so help her…

Clint loped up. "Did they see him?"

Not trusting herself to speak, she shook her head, willing the emotions to pass. Clint rubbed his chin. He seemed nervous, upset.

"Are you okay?" She placed her hand on his arm. The muscles bunched, but she didn't pull away.

"Yeah." The sky grew darker. "I guess I'll check the barns again."

"Let's look behind the cabins. Maybe he wandered back there."

The glance he flashed her said it was a fool's errand, but she didn't care. They trained their flashlights behind the row of cabins. No sign of the dog. Clint's house stood at the end of the drive. The dark windows gave it a sad air, like it was waiting for him to come home.

"Clint, what's that on your front porch?"

He twisted to see and took off toward his house. She ran to catch up with him.

Banjo! Clint knelt next to the dog, massaging his ears. Banjo's tail thumped on the wood, and his tongue hung out. The dog was clearly thrilled to see Clint.

"I thought we'd lost you, old boy," he said.

"I guess he missed you." She leaned her shoulder against the rail, never imagining Clint could look this happy.

He continued lavishing Banjo with affection. "Probably looking for a treat or something."

"He can stay here with you, you know."

"It wouldn't be right." He rose.

"Why not? I can tell you like dogs."

"I've never owned one."

The man whose face lit up like the carnival rides at the rodeo when he saw Banjo had never owned a dog? Impossible.

"He's getting old," Lexi said. "If you don't want him here, that's fine, but if you like him, well…maybe he needs some TLC after long days with the cattle."

"He *is* getting old." Clint straightened, thinking about it. "I've been meaning to mention the ranch should add a few more dogs. I've trained cattle herders. It takes time for them to learn the ropes. If something happens to Banjo…"

"I'll check into it."

He looked as if he wanted to say something, then he shook his head. "I'll walk you home."

"It's not far." She waved the flashlight in the direction of her house. "The boogeyman won't get me."

"I'm walking you home." And there was serious Clint again. Only Banjo seemed to lighten him up. "I know you can take care of yourself. But I'd feel better if..."

Such a small thing, him caring about her safety, but it made her feel warm and toasty. And for the first time in hours, she didn't feel like crying in the slightest.

She'd been right to hire Clint. Nothing escaped his notice on the ranch, not even a sweet old dog.

Careful, Lexi. Start to romanticize him, and you'll end up like last time. In a dull relationship without the things you really want. The ring. The emotional connection. The once-in-a-lifetime love.

Whether she liked it or not, she was the boss, and she'd better not forget it.

Chapter Three

"Storm's coming tonight. I'm heading into town." Clint shifted from one cowboy boot to the other Monday afternoon. "Do you need any supplies?"

"I'll come with you." The words were out of Lexi's mouth before she'd thought them through. She stood in the open doorway as a gust of wind swooshed inside.

She hadn't left the house in three days, and she was losing her mind. Natalie Allen, her vice president and top wedding planner, had taken more responsibilities off Lexi's shoulders, but details continued to slip through the cracks. Lexi was still reeling from the nasty phone call she'd received this morning from a very unhappy client. She couldn't help thinking if she'd been there, the situation could have been prevented.

In his Carhartt jacket, jeans and cowboy hat, Clint looked ready to bolt. "If you give me a list—"

"I want to tag along." She was already pulling on her faux fur–lined boots.

"I have errands to run first."

"Even better." She shrugged into her coat. "Just drop

me off downtown and text me when you're ready to go to the store."

His expression darkened, but he nodded. "I'll be in the truck."

He didn't have time to walk away, because she'd grabbed her purse and followed him outside. With Clint managing the ranch, maybe it was time for her to return to Denver. For good.

She bit the corner of her bottom lip, less than thrilled at the thought.

He opened the passenger door of his black truck for her, and she buckled herself in, thankful the cab was warm.

"So…what's on your agenda?" She watched him adjust the mirrors then back the truck up.

"Dottie will be mad if I don't stop in and say howdy, so I'm headed to her diner first. Then I'm meeting Art McFall about his hay supply. I have to stop in at the bank, and I'm due for a trim."

"Dottie. Hay. Bank. Barber. Got it. How long do you think it will take?"

"Two hours."

Two whole hours.

She watched the bare countryside pass by. It was part of her, the same way selecting complementary colors for a bouquet was part of her. After living in the city for years, she'd never thought she'd miss the raw emptiness of the land, but she did. Was that why the thought of returning to Denver wasn't lighting up her insides?

"I've looked over the ranch's books some more," Clint said. "We'll be selling the calves soon, even though the prices are low."

"Okay." She faced him, remembering the twinge of doubt she'd had at their meeting last week.

"The new barn is empty, and it cost a lot to build."

"I know."

"To fill the barn with square bales next summer, you need farm equipment."

She knew where he was going with this. Equipment cost money.

He concentrated on the road ahead. "If you want the equipment, you need to get a high price for your calves."

A dull ache formed behind her eyes. "You think we should wait a few months to sell, don't you?"

"Not if we can't feed them."

"Can we feed them?" She watched him carefully, trying to read his reaction.

"I think we can."

She weighed her options. If they couldn't feed the cattle, they'd lose even more money than if they sold them soon at a low price.

"Let me think about it more." She waited for him to argue, but his only reaction was a curt nod. Was he mad she hadn't instantly agreed with him?

Maybe these unresolved ranch issues were the reason she wasn't speeding back to her real life. It wouldn't be fair to Clint if she deserted him now. She'd told him she planned to stay until Christmas.

"I can't take chances with the ranch," she said. "Every decision I make is important."

"I understand."

He remained silent as the miles passed. She wished she could tell him to go ahead and do whatever he wanted with the calves, but she had to think about the big picture. Logan and Sarah and their little ones depended on her. As did the other ranch hands. Not to mention the cattle—she wouldn't risk harming them. Preserving the ranch itself loomed heaviest. Would Daddy have approved of Clint's plan?

The lingering silence set her on edge.

"Has Banjo been okay?" she asked.

"He's fine."

Not exactly forthcoming with information, that Clint Romine. What was a safe topic for small talk?

"What are you doing for Thanksgiving?" she asked. "Hard to believe it's only a few days away."

His hands tightened around the steering wheel. "I'll feed the cattle in the morning and later ride out to check on them."

"What about your family?"

"I don't have one."

"What do you mean?" It hadn't occurred to her he'd be spending his Thanksgiving alone, too.

He glanced her way and shrugged. "Dad died in a blizzard back when I was four. Multicar pileup. He drove trucks for a living. Never knew my mom. My grandfather took care of me until I turned six, then he died. I lived in foster homes from then on."

The full impact of his words didn't hit her for a few seconds. When it did, she didn't know what to say. Was he completely alone in life? "Who do you usually spend Thanksgiving with? And Christmas?"

"Thanksgiving isn't a big deal to me. Dottie always invites me to her place, but it's a little too crowded for my liking. As for Christmas, my best friends and I usually get together when we can, but we're all bachelors, all live a cowboy life to some degree..."

"So you spend the holidays alone."

"Yes."

She tapped her legs. He didn't sound bothered at the thought of being alone for Thanksgiving and Christmas. Unlike her.

"Here we are." Clint stopped in a parking spot in front of Dottie's Diner. "I'll text you when I'm done."

"Tell Dottie hello from me." She climbed out of the truck, shoved her hands in her coat pockets and headed toward the jewelry store. Clint's childhood must have been pretty bad for him to spend holidays alone. She'd been blessed to always have Daddy to come home to. Who knew how she'd spend the holidays from now on?

Sweet Dreams was all decked out for Christmas. Rows of buildings—some brick, some with awnings—lined both sides of Main Street, and all were trimmed in green-and-red decorations. White lights wrapped around light posts and store windows. Evergreen boughs and red ribbons abounded. Very Victorian Western. She imagined women in long dresses and bonnets singing carols back in the day. Throw in a cowboy or two, and the picture would be complete.

Lexi ducked into Sweet Dreams Jewelers and instantly felt at home. There was something about jewelry, soft lighting and gleaming glass displays that soothed her. She zoomed to the diamonds showcased on blue velvet. Lingering over the engagement rings, she sighed in delight. The one in the top right corner caught her eye. She'd pick it as her ideal ring. Oh, how she loved weddings.

The recent Anderson nuptials had been particularly moving. The bride and groom had stared into each other's eyes so deeply as they said their vows that Lexi had shed a few honest tears at their devotion. Those moments made her job worth the petty calls, ornery brides, making payroll and endless meetings. Yes, the *I do*s made it all worth it.

After browsing the store, she made her way to Amy's Quilt Shop. Lexi herself had never quilted, but the fabrics might give her ideas for any rustic weddings coming up. The bell clanged above her, and she stopped to take it all in. The aroma of spiced cider and the sounds of soft contemporary Christian Christmas music filled the room, pretty rag rugs in navy blues and brick reds covered the wood floors, and the displays—magnificent! She plunged forward, marveling at the combination of fabrics. The quilts hanging from the walls were works of art.

"Can I help you?"

Lexi turned and squealed. "Amy Deerson? You're Amy's Quilt Shop?"

"Lexi!" Amy embraced her, and they couldn't stop grinning at each other. "I can't believe it. I haven't seen you in years. I'm so sorry about your dad, and I feel terrible I missed the funeral. Stomach flu. If I'd known you were still in town, I would have come over."

"Thank you, Amy. That means a lot to me." Lexi couldn't get over how beautiful Amy had become. Luxurious dark hair tumbled down her back. Full red lips, a fit but curvy figure, and her smile, so inviting and kind. The way she'd always been. Amy had been a good friend during high school, but after Lexi left for college, they'd fallen out of touch.

"Are you busy right now?" Amy asked.

"No, why?"

"Let's catch up over a cup of coffee."

"Can you do that?"

"I sure can. It's my store." Amy laughed. "Give me a minute and we can go to The Beanery."

A short walk later, they sat across from each other at a café table in the adorable coffee shop. Exposed brick walls contrasted with distressed plank floors. The way the door opened every few minutes told Lexi it was a popular place indeed. And the smell was pure coffee, pure bliss.

"Fill me in on everything." Amy sipped her pumpkin spice latte and leaned forward.

Lexi obliged. She told her about earning her degree in public relations and getting her first gig as a wedding planner. She'd quickly made a name for herself, quit her job and started planning weddings full-time. Then a swanky Denver magazine featured her in their wedding issue, and the business exploded. "Your turn."

"There's not much to tell. I opened shop six years ago. Let's just say I was on the verge of getting engaged twice and both times got jilted. I'm finally coming to terms with the fact I might never marry or have children. I've been spending time working on my relationship with the Lord."

Lexi's heart twisted at Amy's tale. Her vibrant friend had always been nurturing. If anyone should be married with kids, Amy should. "I need to do some of that myself."

"Which part?" Amy teased.

"The last part. Losing Daddy…it's been hard." She sipped her coffee.

"I can't imagine," Amy said. "How long did you know about the cancer?"

"I didn't. None of us did." She blotted a napkin over the drop she'd spilled. Something about the question bothered her. Had anyone else known?

Had Daddy known?

No. If he'd known, he would have told her. He'd been as in the dark as everyone else.

"Maybe that's a blessing. He didn't suffer."

Lexi didn't see how it was a blessing, but she wouldn't argue. If they'd had more time, they could have fought it.

Amy smiled warmly. "Looks like you're making big changes in your life. I'll pray for you."

"I need all the prayers I can get. I think God's mad at me." She half laughed.

Amy covered her hand and squeezed. "He's not mad at you, Lexi. You can go to Him with anything, big or small."

"Thanks, Amy," she whispered. Her phone dinged. Clint. "Well, it's been wonderful to catch up with you, but my ride is almost here. Let's get together soon."

"Here's my number. Let me know if you need anything."

They hugged, and Lexi left, wrapping her coat tightly around her waist against the cold air. Amy's words about going to God with anything filled her thoughts.

In the past, she'd trusted God with her plans. But she'd gotten busy with her company, and after her father died…

Was she being punished? She'd put her business first and lost him a month after planning her most prestigious wedding. She'd been named homecoming queen two weeks before her mother died. Whenever something wonderful happened to her, she paid a price too heavy to bear.

Could she take anything to God in prayer?

Lord, I want to believe You listen to my prayers. Am I foolish to stay here until Christmas? Should I go back to Denver? And what should we do about the calves?

She shook her head. Why would God care if she stayed or left or sold the calves now or later?

Do You really care? About things big and small?

Clint's truck drove into the spot directly in front of her. That man did everything he said he would do. He was reliable. A hard worker. And in her heart she knew he was right about them needing a higher price for the calves. Owning a business meant taking calculated risks.

She buckled into the passenger seat. "I think we should try it your way and wait to sell the calves."

He blinked. Then he nodded, a sheepish smile playing on his lips. "Okay."

One decision out of the way. Her business would not collapse if she stayed here until Christmas. One more month. Then she'd figure out the rest.

Clint hauled plastic bags full of groceries into Lexi's kitchen later that afternoon. Walking into this house was like getting a hearty slap to the face each and every time he came in. The dripping of the faucet pounded into his temples. The wind had picked up, flapping the broken screen. And how had he not noticed the bulb missing in the can light above him?

Here he was living in the lap of luxury in his cozy home down the lane, and Lexi was stuck in this rundown tomb of a house.

The minute he'd moved into his cabin, he'd scrubbed it and checked the windows, furnace and plumbing. He'd tightened the place up good for winter, and every room sparkled like sunlight off the river.

If anyone but Lexi lived here, he probably would assume they'd fix it up themselves, but this was a woman who had lost both parents, held a demanding job and didn't have a boyfriend or husband to rely on.

Which left him responsible.

Repairs would put him in Lexi's direct vicinity far longer than he could handle. Even if he could admit—at least to himself—he didn't mind making chitchat with her. It wasn't conducive to keeping their relationship professional, though. And now that she'd actually trusted his decision about the calves, his palms wouldn't stop sweating.

What if he was wrong? What if they ran out of feed and had to sell them for a loss?

He closed his eyes and shook away the doubts. It was too late for regrets now. He'd show Lexi her faith in him wasn't misplaced. And he'd start today.

"Lexi?"

"Hmm?" She pushed a jar to the side and shoved a box of cereal onto the shelf.

"I've noticed there are some items around here that need fixing. I'm busy tonight—have to check the generators and equipment before the snow comes in—but tomorrow night, I'll come by and get a few of the more pressing problems repaired."

Lexi wiped her palms down her jeans. "What problems?"

Was she joking?

From the expression on her face, he'd say she wasn't. "I hear a faucet dripping somewhere. It might be an easy fix, or it might need a new gasket or have to be replaced altogether. The screen in the window—" he pointed to the living room "—is ripped and banging around in the wind. Your fireplace needs to be inspected." He turned in a slow circle, seeing cobwebs, a loose cabinet knob, an electrical outlet missing its cover.

With her hands on her hips, she scrunched her nose and studied the rooms. "It's needed a cleaning for a long time. I didn't realize there were so many other issues, though."

Understandable with her father dying and her business keeping her so busy.

"After my mother died when I was seventeen, I think Daddy gave up on the house. He lived here, but he poured all his time and energy into the ranch itself. Maybe he was afraid of moving on, or he could have thought changing the house would make him forget her." She bowed her head. "I haven't been blind to it being so dirty. I just haven't had the energy… You must think I'm a slob."

"No, I figured you've been busy."

She smiled up at him, and he held his breath. She had a knight-in-shining-armor glint in her eyes. "I would appreciate it very much if you'd stop by tomorrow night. I'll do my best to help."

He was no knight.

"I can manage fine."

She tilted her head, still smiling. "I know you can. But it's my house. And I'd feel like the worst sort of person if I let you do it all without lifting a finger."

An image of Lexi holding a wrench and him accidentally touching her hand made him squirm. She was too pretty to be near for long periods.

"I said I can manage."

"And I said I'll help."

He clamped his mouth shut. He couldn't argue with her without sounding like a grizzly bear. He hoped the faucet was an easy fix. The screen and fireplace, too.

Because if she started helping, she'd start talking, and when she talked, he had a hard time remembering why he needed to keep his distance.

And he needed to keep his distance. For both their sakes.

Lexi paused in front of the master bedroom door the next evening. She'd made too big of a deal out of Daddy's room. She knew what she'd find—the double bed with a faded blue-and-yellow quilt, dusty dressers with her father's personal items on a tray. Why had she been avoiding it for so long?

Slowly, she opened the door. His presence hit her, the faintest smell of cologne lingering. The bed, the quilt, the dusty dresser were the same. She crept to the tray with her dad's belongings and gingerly picked up his watch. It had been a gift to him from her mother. He'd worn it every day Lexi could remember. It looked so out of place and lonely sitting here instead of wrapped around his wrist. Tears filled her eyes, and she gripped it tightly to her chest.

This was why she hadn't gone in. It reminded her too much of him.

Swallowing her emotions, she clutched the watch in one hand and trailed her finger over the rest of the surfaces, stopping at the framed picture of her parents on their honeymoon. Daddy's arm was slung over Mama's shoulders, and they looked so happy and young. *How I wish you were still here.*

She'd loved both of them so much. It didn't seem possible they were gone. Slowly, she turned, taking in the room, trying to hold on to the memory of his smile, the sound of his laugh, the feel of his arms pulling her into a hug. *Oh, Daddy, I miss you.*

The top drawer of her mother's dresser was slightly ajar. She pulled it open. A file had been placed on top of old scarves. She lifted it out, but a knocking sound from the front door made her jump. Quickly, she wiped her eyes, and with the file in hand, she hurried back to the living room and let Clint inside. Snowflakes flurried around him. He tapped his hat on his leg before entering.

"You look cold." Her spirits lifted now that he'd arrived. "And, wait, are you smiling?"

His teeth flashed in a grin as he set his tool belt on the floor to take off his coat and boots. "I love this weather. It's not blowing too hard, and the cows are munching away as the snow piles up on them. I hope you don't mind, I dallied a few minutes to take some pictures."

"You? Dallied?" She padded down the hall with him at her heels. "I'm shocked. And here I pegged you as all business all the time."

She stopped to face him, and he bumped into her. His hands shot to her biceps, his touch warming her down to the tips of her icicle toes.

"I pegged you as the same." His dark blue eyes flashed with intensity.

She felt aware of him in a way she hadn't previously. She wanted to lean into his muscular frame, let him take away the sorrow of losing her father. Instead, she stepped back, forcing a laugh. "You pegged me right, then. Let's see those photos."

His face blanked. "You want to see my pictures?"

"Well, yeah." She shook her head. "Why wouldn't I?"

Color flooded his cheeks, but he swiped his phone and held it out. Two cows stared at her, both munching on hay, an inch of snow on their backs. The sky was white behind them.

"This picture is really good, Clint." She pulled the phone closer to get a better look. "They seem content."

"That's what I thought." The moment stretched, and he cleared his throat. "Where is the bathroom? I suspect the dripping is coming from that sink."

She showed him to the room, and she stood in the doorway as he turned on the faucet and opened the cabinet to check the pipes. "What can I do?"

"Nothing."

"Clint…"

He glanced up at her. "Well, you can show me where the water main is."

"Oh, that might be a problem. I don't know where it is."

"I'll find it." His eyes danced with amusement.

He was easy to be with. Not much of a talker, but she liked him just the same. Her thoughts bounced to two days from now, Thanksgiving, and how they were both alone with nowhere to go.

Didn't it made sense to ask him to join her? Yes, it was taking a risk. Spending time together meant further developing a friendship. If something happened to end the friendship, he might quit. She had to keep the ranch's welfare number one in her priorities. But the loneliness of this upcoming holiday enveloped her.

They were both adults. Surely they could have a meal with each other without their working relationship blowing up.

Clint straightened and moved toward the door.

"Wait, I have a question for you." She touched his arm, all firm muscle, then snatched her hand back. "Why don't you have Thanksgiving dinner with me?"

"I have plans."

She cocked her head to the side. "You told me you were feeding the cattle."

"Yes. Those are my plans."

"You can't feed cattle all day."

He didn't look at her.

"Come on." She sighed. "Neither of us has family, and I don't want to go to a well-meaning friend's house, if you know what I mean."

He met her eyes, understanding connecting them before he moved past her into the hall. "I thought you don't cook."

"I don't. I can buy a premade dinner from the supermarket."

"Where's the utility room?"

She tried not to let her disappointment show as she gestured for him to follow her past the living room and kitchen to the door next to the garage. Clint gravitated toward the pipes against the wall. His lack of interest in her offer was apparent. And that was fine. She'd been thinking of him as a friend when she should be thinking of him as the ranch manager.

She'd spend Thanksgiving alone. Maybe she'd drive somewhere, eat Chinese food or something. She didn't *have* to spend it here.

"If I eat Thanksgiving dinner with you," he said over his shoulder, "we're not having supermarket food. We're going to cook it. I'll show you the basics."

"Really?" Had the sun suddenly appeared? Were rainbows arching over the house? "Thank you! But cooking isn't my strong suit. The basics might be beyond me."

He cranked a lever on a copper pipe. "Something tells me you'll pick it up quickly. Now, stay in here while I turn on the faucet. If I yell to turn it off, pull this lever up, okay?"

She nodded, admiring his broad back as he left the room. Only then did she realize she was still holding the file she'd found in her mother's drawer. Absentmindedly, she opened it, scanning the sheet.

Her mouth dropped open. Heart stopped beating. Vision blurred.

Clint ran back into the utility room, yanking the lever up. "Didn't you hear me calling?"

She lifted her face, the file and its contents dropping to the floor, each sheet gliding in a different direction.

"He lied to me, Clint. He lied. He knew." Everything she'd thought to be true since the funeral suddenly came into question. And the betrayal almost buckled her knees.

He placed his hands on her shoulders and peered into her eyes. "Who? What are you talking about?"

"Daddy knew he had cancer, and he didn't tell me."

Chapter Four

Clint had no idea what to do, so he bent and picked up the papers that had scattered across the floor. He scanned the top sheet. Pathology report. Dated October 1 of this year. A handwritten note about getting a second opinion was scrawled in the margin.

"He must not have known for long. A month, tops." Clint handed her the papers, but she kept her arms by her sides, her hands balled into fists.

"He kept this from me." Her words were tight, cold, hard. "He robbed me of helping him."

"I'm sorry—"

"The faucet will have to wait. I need to be alone."

Clint nodded, set the documents on a shelf and left. His thoughts were jumbled as he strode under the dark sky back to his cabin. Lexi had so many dimensions. He'd seen her exhausted, mourning, professional, playful and now this. Whatever this was. Upset didn't quite explain it.

Betrayed, most likely. It was the lying part she'd focused on.

And the lying part was something he knew a little too well.

A pit formed in his stomach. He'd been keeping something from her, too. But what could he do about it now? She was already reeling from her father's death. Finding out RJ had known about the cancer had put her over the edge. If Clint came clean and told her about how he lost his property, it would add to her burdens. She'd fire him and be left without a manager. She'd work night and day to save this ranch as well as her company, and she'd be as hollowed out as she'd been when she hired him.

It wouldn't be right to add to her problems to selfishly clear his conscience.

He ducked his chin against the snow pellets. Why was she so upset about her dad not telling her, anyhow? A month seemed pretty quick to go from diagnosis to death. Maybe RJ had planned on filling her in at Thanksgiving. Or maybe he thought he was invincible. From all accounts, he sounded like the kind of guy Clint had been surrounded by his entire adult life—a tough Wyoming rancher who never admitted defeat, not even to cancer.

Regardless, Clint and Lexi weren't close. They'd only known each other a short time. Not telling her about his past wasn't a betrayal. He was doing what she'd hired him to do—managing the ranch.

Speaking of which… He hadn't secured additional feed for the winter. If he didn't find any in the next week or so, they would have to sell the calves at the scheduled date or risk losing valuable cattle in the frigid months ahead.

Was he making the best decisions for the ranch? Maybe he'd been lying to himself and his past *was* affecting his work performance.

His porch light glowed, and he muttered under his breath at the sight of Banjo curled up on the welcome mat the same way he'd been every night since Clint had found him there last Thursday. Each night he'd tried to take the dog back to the barn, but Banjo wouldn't budge from the porch.

"We've got to stop meeting like this." Clint bent to stroke Banjo's black-and-white fur, and the dog got to his feet, wagging his tail and adoring Clint with his big brown eyes. "This isn't your home. You can't stay here."

Banjo cocked his head.

"Fine. I can't have you freezing. You can sleep on the floor. Just this once." He unlocked the door. He'd said those same words every night, and *just this once* had turned into *Banjo, you own me*. "Okay, I'll admit I'm a pushover. But you are sleeping on the floor."

The idea of Banjo sleeping on the end of his bed appealed to him, but he couldn't allow it. He didn't want the dog living with him. Banjo was old, arthritic, and Clint doubted he would make it through the next year. Growing attached to the dog would not be smart. He'd lose him, too.

Clint took off his coat and boots and stretched out on the couch. Banjo lay on the rug.

It felt as if every hour brought a new set of issues to deal with. Banjo. The faucet still not repaired. And Thanksgiving with his boss.

She was probably too upset to celebrate Thanksgiving now. He should be relieved, but part of him hoped otherwise.

His cell phone dinged, showing a text from Lexi.

I'm sorry I flipped out. Please send me the list of ingredients I need to buy for our Thanksgiving dinner.

Had she read his mind? "Guess Thanksgiving is still on." He texted her back.

I'll buy everything tomorrow. See you Thursday.

Leaning back, he tried to relax. He hadn't had this much excitement in years. He tried to avoid drama. But the anticipation kicking up his pulse didn't lie. He kind of liked drama of the Lexi variety. Maybe a little excitement wasn't such a bad thing after all.

She would be on her best behavior with Clint today. This Thanksgiving would be difficult enough without Daddy. If she scared Clint off, she'd be alone with only her thoughts to keep her company. They kept circling like buzzards over roadkill. Why hadn't Daddy told her about the cancer? She deserved to know. Hadn't he understood she would want to rush home and be with him?

Stop fixating on it. It's over.

She slid a dusty platter into the soapy dishwater. Her mother's fine china stayed in the hutch most of the year. Lexi had always loved the blue-and-white set. Rinsing the platter, she could almost smell her mother's perfume and hear her laughter. Mama had been such a joyful, optimistic person, and Lexi had been close to her until she died from complications due to pneumonia.

And now Daddy was gone, too.

Tuesday night after she'd basically kicked Clint out, she'd stood in the utility room, trying to make sense of the pathology report, hearing Clint's words about not knowing for long. But the report had made her paranoid. Who else wasn't telling her vital information? Had

Daddy confided in someone other than her? The mere thought sliced her heart open.

Had she been the only one *not* to know?

While her father had had many acquaintances, the one person she could imagine him confiding in besides her was Jerry. Yesterday morning, she'd asked Jerry if he'd known about the cancer, and from the expression on his face, she'd believed his hearty no. Who else would Daddy tell? His brother had died five years ago, and he didn't have any other close friends.

Clint arrived carrying several bags of groceries.

"Happy Thanksgiving." She hurried to the hallway and reached for one of the bags.

"Here, take this one. It's not as heavy."

She peeked inside. A Dottie's Diner box labeled pumpkin pie. Her mouth began watering. As they unpacked the groceries in the kitchen, a charged silence filled the air. She had to say something, but she didn't want to discuss her dad or her reaction to the pathology report.

"What should I do?" she asked.

"Do you have a roasting pan?" All business, Clint washed his hands. "I bought a turkey breast instead of an entire bird. We'll rub butter on it and sprinkle it with salt and pepper. It will cook pretty quick."

Some of her tension leaked out. "What does a roasting pan look like?"

"Rectangular with a wire rack inside." He rinsed the turkey breast and patted it dry with a paper towel.

She searched through the cupboards and finally found a pan fitting the description. "Is this it?"

"Yes." He smiled then, and she couldn't help but stare. He wasn't a man who smiled often. Catching a glimpse of it felt like being let in on a spectacular secret. It made her want to find out more of his secrets. Who was this man? Why was he single? Had he ever been in love? Married? And why had he been working at an oil company for years when he clearly loved ranching?

"Put this in the microwave for twenty seconds." He handed her half a stick of butter.

Her questions were too personal. If she asked him the real stuff, she might not like the answers.

"How did you learn to cook?" She pushed the microwave button and leaned against the counter, watching him pull out cutting boards, knives and salt and pepper as if he lived there.

"Food Network."

She laughed, trying to picture him watching cooking shows. The image didn't mesh with the outdoorsy cowboy in front of her. He drew near, standing inches from her. What was he doing? Her heart pounded. But he simply reached around her to turn on the oven.

"I can't see you glued to the TV and taking notes."

Was a blush creeping up his cheeks? She didn't even try to conceal her glee.

"I don't. I got snowed in for a week. I was bored. Nothing was on television, and one of the cooking shows made me hungry. I decided to try my hand at the recipe. I got hooked."

"Well, I'm glad you did. The soup you made for me was delicious."

"Bring the butter over." He brandished a pastry brush and demonstrated how to paint the butter on the meat. "You want to cover the entire thing."

She swiped the melted butter on the skin, and Clint sprinkled salt and pepper over it before sliding the pan into the oven.

"Easy enough, right?" He pointed to the items she'd grouped together on the counter. "You peel potatoes, and I'll chop the herbs and vegetables for the stuffing."

The sound of the knife hitting the board in precise thuds filled the air. She took her time peeling each potato and rinsing them. Now that Clint was here, her mind wasn't racing in tangled circles about her father. But other problems loomed. Yesterday, she'd called Natalie Allen, vice president of her company, and the conversation had left her perplexed. Something wasn't right in Denver.

"Do you ever question people's motives?" She lined the potatoes up on the board and turned to face him.

"Why do you ask?" The muscles in his shoulders flexed as he chopped celery.

"I talked to my vice president yesterday afternoon. She's been meeting with the other wedding planners, and she told me they think I should hire a purchaser to keep up with ordering the invitations, flowers, decorations and such."

"Who orders the stuff now?"

"The planners are responsible for their weddings. They rely on their assistants for most of the ordering."

"Can your company afford another full-time employee?"

The company could, but keeping up with the orders hadn't been a problem until she'd moved to Wyoming.

"Yes, but it's never been an issue before. In the past I've trusted Natalie had the best interests of the company in mind with her decisions. But I'm wondering if something more is going on. Something she isn't telling me."

"Why would you think that?"

The missed orders, the complaints. Lexi had always

checked in with the wedding planners once a week. But since living at the ranch, she wasn't able to spend time with the individual employees the way she used to. Natalie had taken on the responsibility. Strange that no one had ever brought up needing a purchaser before. Was she overreacting?

"I guess finding the pathology report made me a little paranoid. Just because my father kept something important from me doesn't mean everyone else is, too."

Clint swept all of the tiny bits of onion, celery and sage into a large bowl. "What would you do if she *was* hiding something?"

"My company comes first. If Natalie doesn't know that by now… Forget it. It doesn't matter, because she's honest with me. Like I said, the other night messed with my head." She wiped her hands on a paper towel. "What do I do now?"

His eyes met hers, and for a brief moment she wondered if he was hiding something, too.

Don't look for the worst in everyone.

"Cut them into small pieces and put them in here." He pointed to a large pot.

Lexi cut the potatoes up in chunks, mentally chastising herself. He was a hard worker, a great ranch manager. He'd gone to the trouble of buying this food, and he was teaching her how to cook it. The idea Clint was hiding something from her was laughable.

She'd nip this suspiciousness in the bud. It wasn't her style. If she couldn't trust the people she worked closely with, she didn't know what she would do.

He couldn't remember a Thanksgiving dinner he'd enjoyed more. Even the delicious feasts Dottie Lavert used to cook at Yearling Group Home didn't compare to this. It wasn't that the food tasted better, although it was delicious. Today was the first time he'd felt like he belonged somewhere on Thanksgiving.

"Dinner was yummy." Lexi closed the door to the dishwasher and pressed the start button. "I'm stuffed. As much as I want pumpkin pie, I think I need to wait awhile for dessert."

"Same here." Now what? Dinner was over, so should he leave? Then he remembered the faucet. "I'll finish fixing the leak in your faucet, then I'll get out of your hair."

"Oh, don't worry about the faucet." She waved dismissively. "And you're not in my hair."

She didn't seem in a rush to get rid of him, but now that she'd mentioned hair, he found himself mesmerized by her silky dark waves. His thoughts detoured to a less professional place than he'd prefer. "It's no trouble. I'll fix it now."

Fifteen minutes later, after tightening the faucet's adjusting ring, he returned to the living room, where Christmas music played.

He cleared his throat. "You're all set. Thanks for having me."

"Wait." She sprang to her feet, her eyes darting back and forth. "I have another favor to ask, but you don't have to say yes."

"What is it?" He wanted to stay. Liked being here with her. The Christmas music reminded him of movies he used to watch with happy families celebrating the holidays. Hanging out with her, listening to the music, almost made him believe he could experience a taste of the happy Christmas feeling, too.

"Would you help me bring down our Christmas tree?

It's in the garage attic with the other decorations. I can pull the bins out myself, but the tree is heavy."

"I'll bring it down." A surge of masculine pride filled his chest. It was nice to be needed for something.

On the way to the garage, Lexi chattered about old decorations and the pink lights she'd ordered for her tree in Denver. Pink lights? Sounded like Lexi. He climbed the attic ladder first, tugging on the lightbulb string when he reached the top. Lexi bumped into him on her way up, and he moved to the side, steadying her.

Standing so close to her messed with his head. Warm, feminine, smelling fantastic—she was special, all right.

"I think the decorations are over here. It's been years since I helped decorate, and I never had to bring them down. Daddy might have moved them." Carefully, she made her way to the corner, where shelves held bins and boxes. "Wow, I can't believe all this is here. My mom used to plan themed trees. She got such a kick out of picking the perfect ornaments and color schemes. These boxes—" she turned to him, her eyes shining "—they're all her Christmas tree themes. Daddy must have saved them. Oh, there's what I was looking for!"

"Which one?" He saw four long boxes clearly marked as artificial trees.

"On the top. It's prelit. He bought it a few years ago. Why he hung on to the old trees is a mystery."

Clint took the long box by the handles and effortlessly brought it down the ladder and back to the living room. Lexi followed with a plastic bin. Back and forth, they brought down all the boxes she wanted.

"Thank you so much." She wiped dust off her sweater. "When do you usually decorate? Thanksgiving weekend is my favorite time."

"I, uh—" he massaged the back of his neck "—I don't decorate."

She gaped at him. "What do you mean you don't decorate?"

"Well, I don't see much point." Why did he feel like a high school freshman about to fail an important math test? "I don't entertain."

"But it's not just for entertaining. It's for you to enjoy. To capture the glorious spirit of Christmas."

Glorious? Christmas had never been very good for him.

"I have a great idea. Let's go decorate your cabin." She gestured to the garage. "We have extra trees. And I know the perfect decorations for you. Mom went through a cowboy Christmas stage when I was in middle school. I saw the boxes up there."

"What? No. What are you doing?" She had already disappeared down the hall. He tried again. "I don't see the point—"

"This is what I do. I love to decorate. You're going to be thrilled with the results!" She looked back over her shoulder at him and winked.

The wink shut him up. He never knew what he was in for when he spent time with Lexi Harrington. One thing he'd learned? If she got something in her head, he might as well play along, because she did not let go of an idea easily.

They spent the next half hour piling the boxes on the bed of the truck. The wind was blowing, and it was cold out, but it wasn't snowing. As he drove them to his cabin, he kept glancing over at her. She wore a red stocking hat with a pom-pom on top, matching red scarf and a black jacket. Her cheeks were flushed.

When they arrived at his cabin, he hauled two boxes into the living room.

"First, let's get some music cranking." She set a small speaker on the counter and found a Christmas playlist on her phone. Then she unwound her scarf, brought her palms together and pointed to the living room with them. "Okay, think about where you want the tree."

"You decide. I'll get the boxes." He had to escape. Having her in his cabin made the atmosphere too cozy. Outside he breathed in the crisp, cold air and yanked two boxes from the truck. Then he set them next to the fireplace and repeated the process with the artificial tree.

Lexi stood behind the couch, facing the window and holding her hands up as if creating a picture frame. "Is that everything?"

He nodded, stripping off his gloves and coat.

"The tree would look really good right in front of the window here, and you'll be able to see the lights from outside."

"Whatever." He didn't mean to sound uninterested or gruff, but he wasn't used to this. Wasn't used to having a woman in his space or someone caring enough to help him decorate his home. He wasn't used to trimming Christmas trees or listening to merry music with a pretty girl. He couldn't think straight.

He was ready to tell her he could decorate it himself, but she was already on her knees, digging through one of the boxes.

"This is the one time I'm actually glad my dad wouldn't get rid of anything." She held an extension cord up triumphantly. "There's a timer for the lights in here, too." She pulled out colored lights and other odds and ends. "Why don't you start putting the tree together—over there—and I'll organize all the decorations."

Clint scratched his chin. He'd never put a tree together, but it couldn't be too hard. With a shrug, he opened the box and began to stack individual branches of fake balsam on the floor. "Where are the directions?"

"There should be colors painted on the ends of each branch. Put the poles together, then stick the branches in the colored sections. It's easier if you start from the bottom. And fluff the branches as you go."

He sighed and did as he was told. As the tree took shape, he stopped telling himself having Lexi here was a big mistake. Maybe it was the upbeat country version of "Rudolph the Red-Nosed Reindeer" or the seven-foot tree before him. Whatever it was, he wanted the festive feeling to last.

"Nice job." Lexi stood next to him, and he was aware of her in a way he hadn't allowed himself to be previously. She wasn't short, but she was shorter than him. Slender, too. And everything about her seemed to sparkle—from her shiny hair to her red-and-white-striped socks. "Let's wrap a few strands of lights around this. Then we can do the fun part."

The fun part? Having her here was fun. He doubted it could get better.

They draped and tucked the lights around the branches of the tree, getting tangled a few times in the process, but before long, the tree was lit. Lexi set the timer to go on at five every night and to turn off at midnight. Then she plugged it in.

"Ooh...it's pretty." Her hands were on her hips, and a soft smile played on her lips.

"It sure is." He hoped she didn't know he was talking about her. She was the prettiest thing he'd ever seen.

"Let's get the horseshoes and lassos on here." She clapped her hands and grabbed a pile of miniature lassos with red bows on top.

He squinted at the other piles. Horseshoe ornaments, mini cowboy hats and— "What are the red bandannas for?"

"We'll tie them to the ends of some of the branches." She peeked from around the tree, where she was on her tiptoes hooking an ornament.

"Here, let me." He sidled up next to her, gently taking the ornament from her hand and placing it near the top of the tree. Sensing her sharp intake of breath, he stepped back quickly. Didn't want to crowd her or make her uncomfortable. Plus, he had a prickly feeling, as if he might do something weird, like touch her hair. "I'll put the horseshoes up."

He kept his distance as they continued decorating.

"I've saved the best for last." Lexi plucked something out of a bin and hid it behind her back. "Are you ready for this?"

"What is it?" What was she up to now?

She held out a straw cowboy hat. "It's the tree topper. Go ahead, put it on top."

He laughed. "I might not know much about decorating, but I've never heard of a cowboy hat on top. Isn't it supposed to be a star?"

"Not on a cowboy Christmas tree. The hat is the finishing touch." She grinned, holding it out to him.

Smiling, he shook his head and set it up top.

They stepped back to survey their work. He never would have thought of decorating a tree with lassos and horseshoes. With the colored lights, cowboy ornaments and red bandannas tied here and there, it represented him and all he stood for. Something shifted inside him. Softened his heart.

It was his first Christmas tree, and it suited him perfectly. And it was all because of Lexi.

She turned to him, holding up her hand. "Nice work, Romine."

He high-fived her, wanting to express how much this day meant to him but not knowing how. "Wouldn't have happened without you, boss."

"Come on. Pumpkin pie is waiting for us."

Pumpkin pie, Christmas decorating, laughter and music? He'd better not get used to this. The illusion of home had devastated him too many times in the past. He couldn't handle losing another one.

Chapter Five

Lexi craved a good sermon and familiar hymns. She couldn't face her problems alone anymore, and that meant spending more time with God. The good sermon and hymns were easy to find in the postcard-worthy church just outside Sweet Dreams. The spending more time with God, on the other hand, couldn't be rushed.

She made her way up the church aisle. Glancing to her left, she caught sight of Clint. In a button-down shirt and dark jeans, he looked right at home. Her spirits lifted. Whenever he was around, her loneliness eased. She scooted down the pew and sat next to him. He smelled masculine, like aftershave. "I didn't know you went to church here."

"Doesn't everyone?" He craned his neck to take in the people behind them.

"Good point." She opened the service bulletin, ridiculously grateful he was here. The thought of attending church with him every week appealed. "There's no sense in both of us driving. Next time, we should carpool."

A frown was his reply.

"I merely mentioned it to save gas," she whispered. It

wasn't as if she was asking him to donate a kidney. She didn't like driving on icy roads, nor did she enjoy trying to control her car when the high winds blew. It wasn't because she craved his company or anything. "It's silly to take two vehicles."

Again, he didn't make a peep. The man was very independent, which was a nice way to say stubborn. She pursed her lips. Okay, maybe she did crave his company, but she wouldn't beg.

The service started, and she forced her attention away from Clint to sing the opening hymn.

The pastor rose. "Today's sermon text comes from the Gospel according to John, chapter fourteen. The night before He was crucified, Jesus comforted His disciples, telling them, 'Do not let your hearts be troubled. You believe in God; believe also in Me. My Father's house has many rooms…'"

Lexi straightened. Her heart *was* troubled. The past two months had brought a lot of anxiety into her life. Just because she believed in Jesus didn't mean she'd never worry, did it?

"He wanted the disciples to understand that this world and its problems are fleeting. We have an eternal home waiting for us. A room prepared in our Father's house."

Daddy was in one of those rooms. Her throat tightened, and she closed her eyes, wishing she could talk to him. What would she say? *Why didn't you tell me the instant you found out about the cancer? Why did you keep it from me? I had no idea you were sick and going to die. We would have gone to specialists and gotten you treatment.*

Even her imaginary conversations with Daddy were full of judgment and finger-pointing. If she had another chance to talk to him, would she really waste it reprimanding him?

"Are you okay?" Clint whispered.

Only then did she realize she'd rolled her bulletin into a tight scroll and her knuckles had turned white as she gripped it.

"I'm fine."

The service continued, and she kept hearing the words *Do not let your hearts be troubled.* Her heart was a tangled mess. How could it not be?

She tried to concentrate on the service. By the time the collection plate was being passed around, she realized her dreams were changing. What used to be her passion—Weddings by Alexandra—felt more like a burden. She lowered her head, her heart shrinking. Who was she without her company? Without her father?

Lord, I don't know who I am anymore.

The congregation rose. "Our Father..."

Lexi recited the prayer, the words hitting her. She was God's child. She braced her hands against the top of the pew. *Lord, thank You for reminding me I'm Yours. I'll always be Yours. Everything else can be taken from me, but no one can take You from me.*

After another hymn, everyone filed out. Clint took her by the elbow as they emerged into the winter air. His simple touch almost undid her.

"I'll drive next week." He tipped his hat to her and strode away.

With her hands in her coat pockets, she watched him until he got into his truck. He'd been exactly what she'd needed ever since she hired him. *Thank You, God, for sending Clint when I needed someone to depend on.*

"I thought I saw you inside." Amy Deerson approached. "Are you busy? Want to have breakfast with me?"

"I would love to have breakfast with you." Lexi unzipped her purse to find her keys. "Just what I need right now."

Amy beamed. "We can eat out or have scones and coffee at my place."

"Scones would be amazing."

"I live above the store. Come to the back entrance. I'll meet you there."

After letting her car warm up, Lexi drove to Amy's Quilt Shop. She entered the back of the building, climbed the steps and knocked on the wooden door, which Amy opened wide.

"Come in." Dark hardwood floors, tall windows and strings of Edison-style lightbulbs gave the large space a warm, modern feel. Fabrics were stacked by colors in wooden cubbies, and two sewing machines stood side by side on a long table against the wall. A large quilting frame displayed a partially finished quilt in traditional Christmas colors. Lexi had to forcibly refrain herself from touching the exquisite design.

"Amy, this is stunning. Do you make all the quilts you sell?"

"Most of them. I consign three other local quilters' pieces, too." She took plates out of a cupboard in the kitchen area opposite the work space. A round table with four chairs anchored the kitchen, and nearby a couch and love seat faced an entertainment center filled with books and a television. "Have a seat. The coffee won't take long."

"How do you find the time to make quilts on top of running the store?" Lexi sat on the couch, admiring the eclectic decor. A colorful photo of horses grazing in the sunset filled an empty wall space, and unlit candles dotted the room.

"Find time? I make time. I love quilting. Designing brings me joy."

What brings me joy? Lexi thought of Clint's face after they decorated his tree. He'd seemed pleased. More than pleased—touched. Making him happy for a little while had brought her joy.

She noticed an open sketchbook on the coffee table. "What's this?"

"Oh, nothing." Amy closed it. "Just doodles. I can't always find the fabric design I envision."

"So you create your own?" An uncomfortable blend of admiration and envy swirled in Lexi's core. Amy made time to do the things she loved. Lexi's life had devolved into an endless checklist of necessary tasks for her company, ones that brought little happiness.

"No, no." Amy waved. "I was sketching. I don't have the credentials to design fabrics."

"You sure could have fooled me."

The coffeemaker beeped, and Amy set a plate of scones on the ottoman and handed Lexi a mug.

"How are you holding up?" Amy bit into a pastry, her big brown eyes watchful, compassionate.

Lexi held the cup between her hands, letting it warm her. "Some days are better than others."

"That's to be expected."

"It is, isn't it?" Lexi wanted to confide in her, but was it too much, too soon? "I'm tired of bitterness keeping me up at night."

"Oh, honey. I'm sorry. Losing your dad—I can't imagine."

"It's not just the fact he's gone." Sitting here in Amy's cozy world felt safe. "Earlier this week, I found out he knew he had cancer and didn't tell me."

"That's terrible!"

"I know." Lexi nodded. "And the sermon this morning is eating at me. 'Do not let your hearts be troubled'? Like I can control it. If Daddy had told me he had cancer, I would have come home. He would have gotten treatment."

Amy crossed one leg over the other as she sipped her coffee. "How long did he know?"

"About a month."

"Hmm..."

"What?" Lexi broke off a piece of scone and popped it in her mouth. Buttery, slightly sweet—the ideal comfort food on a winter morning.

"Well, I totally get why you're mad and all, but a month isn't much. The cancer must have been aggressive. Even with treatment, he might not have had long to live."

"I know. Chemo and radiation might not have cured him. But why didn't he tell me?"

"I wish I had the answer. I know he loved you, and you can be sure he is in Heaven, in one of those rooms prepared just for him."

I don't want him in Heaven. I want him here.

She missed him. Plain and simple. And maybe that's why she couldn't let it go. She changed the subject, and soon they were laughing about old times. But underneath it all, dissatisfaction lingered. She'd lost her dad. She could very well lose her business. And she didn't know what brought her joy anymore.

The one bright spot was Clint. She didn't have to worry about losing the ranch, too. Not with him running it.

Clint sat in a red vinyl booth at Dottie's Diner, the muffled conversations around him easing the raw edges of his solitude. Being around people, even when he wasn't interacting with them, sometimes made him feel less lonely. Other times, it punctuated how alone he was. Today was a less lonely day. Lexi had a lot to do with it.

"Missed you at Thanksgiving, tiger." Dottie filled his mug with coffee, then set the pot, nearly empty, on the table and slid into the booth opposite him. Her silver hair had poufy bangs in front and was twisted and clipped up in the back. She was a round, kind woman with a sassy tongue and a heart as wide-open as the state of Wyoming. "Every year I ask. Every year you refuse. I hate to think of you alone all the time. It's not natural."

Dottie and Big Bob hosted between thirty and fifty people every holiday. Clint had gone to Thanksgiving there once and had felt out of place. Making small talk with strangers was worse than dealing with an angry bull.

"I wasn't alone." He cautiously sipped the hot coffee, instantly regretting his words. The way her blue eyes started sparkling, he knew he would be forced to give an explanation.

"No?" Her voice climbed an octave. "Who were you with?"

He took another drink, scalding his tongue in the process. Dottie didn't need to know who he'd been with.

"Don't you go getting a burr under your saddle, Clint Romine. I've known you since you were thirteen. Now fess up."

If she blew this out of proportion, he was standing up and leaving, rude or not.

"Lexi Harrington." He quickly added, "She didn't have anyone else."

Her face cleared like the sky after a hard rain. "That's kind of you. I worry about the girl. Losing her daddy and not having her mama around anymore. Plus she's been stuck in the city for years. I don't know how anyone can live like that. People everywhere." She visibly shivered. "You takin' good care of her, hon?"

Was he taking good care of Lexi? He could have asked her if she needed a ride to church this morning. Never mind he hadn't known she was going. And if he had known? He still wouldn't have asked. Decorating his Christmas tree with her had left him wound up tighter than a rope around a wayward calf.

He'd rarely been the center of someone's attention, and Lexi treated him as if he mattered. Thanksgiving—cooking with her and decorating his tree—had shaken him, left him wanting more. More time with her, more of her attention. But if he gave in to the feeling?

She'd change her mind. Realize she'd been vulnerable and spending time with him had been a mistake. She didn't understand he'd always been *that Romine kid*, a worthless brat. If he didn't distance himself, she'd see the truth of who he was, and he didn't want her to think less of him.

Dottie covered his hand with hers. "Where do you go in that handsome head of yours, tiger? You've been doing it ever since I've known you. It's as if you retreat somewhere none of us can find you."

"Sorry." He shook his head. "I'm doing my best at the

ranch. I'm still searching for winter feed to buy. If you hear of anyone willing to sell, give me a call."

"I've been keeping my ears open, but all I hear is the same predicament you're in. Ranchers are looking to buy feed, not sell. Big Bob is at home. Why don't you stop by on your way back? Maybe he's heard something different."

He hoped Big Bob had a lead. If not, Clint would have to sell the calves as soon as possible, take the profit and hope it would be enough to keep the ranch going until next year without having to dip into its cash reserves. The calf sale would be another challenge. It had been years since he'd sold calves, and he'd never done the negotiating.

Why was he worrying? He wouldn't be doing it alone. Jerry would help.

"Thanks, Dottie. I'll do that." He clung to the hope Big Bob had good news for him. He really didn't want to let Lexi down, and not securing additional feed felt like a major failure. He wanted to be more than the worthless Romine kid for once.

Two hours later, Clint marched into the stables, ready to stomp something—anything—in frustration. His chances at feeding the calves along with the cows through the winter were dwindling by the second. Big Bob hadn't known any locals with extra feed for sale. Jerry had no other names to call, and Clint's friends didn't have any leads, either. He'd contacted a ranch in Montana and left three messages, but they'd never returned his calls. It looked like he would have to stick to the original calf sale date in mid-December.

Although it was technically not his duty today, checking on the cattle would take his mind off the fact the ranch wouldn't be buying the farm equipment RJ had wanted to purchase. Clint had a feeling RJ would have secured extra feed, one way or another.

He saddled up his horse and rode into the cold wind. To his surprise, Lexi was atop Nugget and heading toward the gate.

"Where you going?" Clint called.

Lexi expertly turned Nugget to face him. Her lips looked pinched, and even with her winter gear on, she seemed tense. "There's an old cabin northeast of here. Thought I'd check on it."

A cabin? He hadn't seen any cabins. He hadn't explored the property in depth, though. "You're not going by yourself, are you?"

"Why not?"

Why not? Because it's Wyoming and snowstorms kick up at will. Because I don't have the first clue where this cabin is, and I'll worry about you getting dropped by your horse, attacked by an animal or worse, and I'll have no way to find you. "It's not wise to be alone in this weather. I don't want you stranded."

"Well, I can't stay here right now. I'm going. I'll be fine." Under her stocking cap, her hair rippled like silky ribbons, framing her pretty—if agitated—face. Yep, she was ornery. Was she mad he hadn't asked her to come to church with him earlier?

"I'll come with you."

"It's not necessary," she said in crisp syllables.

His first reaction was to retreat, to let her go on her merry way since she obviously didn't want him around, but she'd been kind to him in a way that made him want to protect her. He couldn't let her go off by herself, not if it would put her at risk.

"If you don't want my company, I'll have one of the other hands ride out with you. I don't know where this cabin is, and cell reception is unreliable the farther out you get."

"I'll be fine. See the tree line? There's a winding river beyond it, and trails lead up to the mountains. The cabin is half a mile up on the nearest trail."

"You said trails. If it started to snow and you didn't come back, how would I know which one to take?"

She looked at the ground, considering, and met his gaze. "If you feel compelled to come, then come. It will take a couple of hours, so if you have someplace else to be, then don't bother."

"I don't have any place to be." Clint urged his horse beside hers, and they settled into a steady pace. They rode toward the lodgepole pines in the distance. The clip-clop of the hooves and sound of the wind kept them company for half an hour. He glanced at her often. Why was she mad? Why did she need to get away? Her pink cheeks jutted high as she rode tall and proud. They reached the river she had mentioned, and she gestured for him to follow her. She and Nugget hugged the river until it bent sharply and changed direction.

"The trail is up ahead," she announced, glowering.

"Did I do something to make you mad?"

She didn't reply, and a trail wide enough for both horses appeared as if out of nowhere. With trees breaking the wind, the air felt warmer, and they slowed their pace.

"No," she finally said. "It's not you. I have all these dilemmas in my head, and I don't know what to do with them. I thought getting out of the house, away from the million things on my list, would help."

"And is it helping?"

"Not really. I can't escape from myself."

Strangely, he understood exactly what she meant. He'd tried to escape from himself so many times over the past four years.

"It's been a long time since I thought about what makes me happy," she said. "Riding makes me happy. So that's what I'm doing today."

"But...you're not happy."

"No."

"Why not?" He dreaded her reply. What if he was the reason?

"Let's put it this way—bitter doesn't look good on me."

"Oh." He nodded. "You're still upset about your dad."

"I'm going to call his doctor. Get some answers." She met Clint's gaze, and he nodded, but he wondered if it would help. What answers could the doctor give her?

A small, ancient log cabin came into view. They dismounted and tied the horses to the hitching post nearby. Clint's senses alerted. Last week's snow had melted, and the weather had warmed for two days, but the temperature dropped since then, leaving the ground solid. Lexi reached for the door.

"Wait." He hurried to her side. "Let me go in first."

"Why?"

"Someone's been here recently."

"How can you tell?"

"Footprints." He crouched, pointing to the indentations around the entrance. "These were made during the thaw. The fact they're still here tells me someone stopped by before the temperatures dropped again." He back-tracked to the horses and inspected the area. "No signs of horses, though. I don't know how whoever it was got out here. A four-wheeler would have left tracks, too."

"People use the cabin from time to time. Daddy said an old mountain man must have built it in the late 1800s. It's a haven if someone is hunting and needs a rest. It's never locked."

"Regardless, I'll go in first." He opened the door. It creaked as it swayed inward. Misshapen wood floors, three windows, an old army cot, a cupboard, two wooden chairs, a table and a stone fireplace greeted him. The dust on the floor and table was patchy, as if someone had been there recently. He poked through the cupboard. Two empty liquor bottles were tucked behind a few plates and mugs.

Lexi stood behind him. "Why would there be empty bottles here?"

"I don't know." Clint shifted his jaw. "But I'm going to find out. Looks like someone thinks your cabin is their party house."

She inspected one corner while he mentally added up possible explanations.

"Looks like whoever was here did more than drink-ing." She pointed to the butt of a marijuana cigarette.

"Unacceptable. For anyone to be coming out here and doing this on your property..." He couldn't finish the thought. "I'll get to the bottom of this."

"It was probably some hunters. I doubt it's the first time someone has done this. As long as they don't bother us."

"You don't deserve this."

She placed her hand on his arm, and he pivoted to face

her. Her expression, like her words, was soft, soothing. "Don't be so upset."

"But—"

"As Jerry likes to remind me, cowboys are like wild horses. You never know when one needs to get away, blow off steam, or whatever else Jerry claims. This was probably a one-time thing."

Clint collected the bottles. Lexi claimed it wasn't a big deal, but he wasn't so sure. She walked out of the cabin.

"What if it's someone from the ranch?"

Surprise then distrust flashed in her eyes. "Wouldn't be the first time I was left in the dark. I don't mind someone using the cabin as a refuge or to hunt, but I won't put up with anyone in my employ getting high or drunk on my property."

"I'll look into it." He ground his teeth together as her words singed his raw conscience. How self-righteous could he be? He, too, was keeping her in the dark. And more and more, he wanted to rid himself of the burden. But how could he? She'd fire him and be left alone, vulnerable, with possible drunkards about.

"I went to see my friend after church. You might know her—Amy Deerson. She owns Amy's Quilt Shop. She has the most incredible studio, and I think that's one of the reasons I've been in such a bad mood." Lexi strode to where they'd tied the horses.

He shook his head. His mind was still 100 percent focused on the person using her cabin for illegal activities, and she wanted to talk about old friends?

"She's making time for her joy. My job used to be my greatest joy." Lexi mounted Nugget. Clint made one more quick sweep of the area, didn't see anything out of the ordinary and got back in the saddle.

"You said 'used to be.'" Clint signaled his horse to move forward. Lexi did the same.

"For the past two years, I've been knee-deep in business details. I've had to cut way back on how many weddings I plan. I never set out to be a manager, but I'm afraid that's what I've become."

He frowned. She didn't like managing her business?

"I'm going to have to make some changes, and I might have to go back to Denver sooner than I'd planned. I've worked too hard to build this company to let it fall apart. Maybe I'm expecting too much from my vice president. I don't know."

His mind raced. She…was leaving?

He didn't want her to leave. He liked her here. Liked their weekly meetings and fixing her faucet and listening to her talk.

He liked being near her.

"I'm so glad I can depend on you, Clint. I can't tell you what a relief it is I don't have to worry about the ranch."

How could she say that when they'd just found evidence that he wasn't on top of the ranch? He hadn't even known this cabin existed. What if whoever had used it knew Lexi was alone up at the main house? He'd seen mild-mannered cowboys get aggressive when they'd had too much to drink.

They emerged from the tree-lined path, and he wanted to shout, *Sorry, but you're putting your faith in the wrong guy.*

"When will you go?"

She prodded Nugget to follow the river. "Tonight. I'm getting to the bottom of whatever's going on at Weddings by Alexandra. Let's plan on our usual Thursday morning meeting this week, okay? I should have the answers I need by then."

It would give him a few more days to make a decision about the calf sale. He might not like it, but Denver was the best place for her. He'd have to get used to her not being around eventually. Besides, he'd never be more than a hired hand, and he'd better not forget it.

Chapter Six

Thursday morning, Lexi unpacked linen samples and draped them around her office at the ranch. Odd that driving into the garage last night had filled her with a sense of home she'd lost during the six years she'd lived in Denver. The past three days had been spent talking to her planners and their assistants, and she was no closer to knowing why so many business details were slipping through the cracks, but she knew for certain something bigger was wrong.

When she'd entered the Weddings by Alexandra headquarters, the front desk's fresh flowers—always the palest of pinks—had been replaced with red roses. Three years ago, she'd hired a professional team to help brand Weddings by Alexandra. They'd emphasized the importance of creating a distinctive identity for her business. The color of the flowers, the music playlist in the waiting area, even the stationery had been selected with care. These details set her apart from other wedding planning companies.

She'd also noticed that two of the planners had unopened boxes stacked in their offices when company policy was to check each delivery as it came in, then move the packages to the storage room. When she confronted them, they quickly moved the boxes, but it didn't change the fact the standards she'd put in place were not being met.

Natalie hadn't been in the office, and her phone had gone directly to voice mail. Last night she'd returned Lexi's calls, assuring her she would handle everything. But why had Natalie let things slide in the first place?

Lexi plunged a box cutter through the packing tape of another box. Daddy's doctor still hadn't called her back. She'd called Monday and yesterday. Left messages, too.

Didn't anyone respect her anymore?

She unpacked the linens and folded a dove-gray napkin before placing it on her desk. After spreading a tablecloth over the folding table she'd brought in, she set it with sample plates and flatware. She stepped back, finger on chin, taking it in. Maybe the table would look better with the classic silverware. Every time she put a wedding together, she couldn't help stashing ideas for her own. Blush bridesmaids' dresses. Tons of flowers—white peonies and pale pink roses—everywhere. The most delicate of stemware. Hand calligraphy on the invitations. And a handsome groom who only had eyes for her.

Clint stood in the doorway.

The fork in her hand clattered to the floor. Her cheeks warmed. One of the reasons she'd anticipated coming home last night was the thought of talking to Clint today.

She was living in an alternate reality, one with a gorgeous cowboy who took care of her problems, a reality as flimsy and fleeting as the bubbles wedding guests blew for fun at receptions. And the man before her *was* her employee. An important detail she dared not forget.

Last night she'd prayed about the situation, hoping she'd feel led to keep things light and professional with Clint. Instead, here she was, dropping forks and blushing like a flighty middle schooler the instant he appeared.

"How did the trip go?" He took off his hat and held it between his hands.

She took a moment to get her equilibrium. "It was eye-opening. I'm disappointed. When I'm not around, the standards seem to slip. My vice president assured me she'd take care of it, but it's frustrating. Plus, one of my couples—a March wedding—canceled."

He frowned. "Why?"

"They broke up. The wedding's off."

"I'm sorry to hear that."

"Me, too." Boy, she was all gloom and doom today. *Look at the bright side, Lexi.* "But, hey, a senator's daughter set up a call with me next Wednesday to discuss the possibility of me planning her wedding. Madeline Roth is a high-profile client, good publicity, so I'm glad."

"Next Wednesday, huh." Clint frowned. "That reminds me. The calf sale is scheduled the same day, and I've got some bad news."

Her stomach clenched. She braced herself for whatever was coming.

"The only feed I can find is three times the price it should be. No one else has a surplus to get us through the winter."

The implications were clear, and she didn't like them. "So we have to sell?"

He nodded, regret all over his face. "I have one more lead, but he's not answering my calls, and we're out of time. If we're going to sell the calves, we need to keep our sale date."

It was as if another ten pounds had been added to her already too-full load. Instead of slumping, though, she kept her back straight.

"That's too bad." She tucked her hair behind her ear. "After looking at your spreadsheet, I'd hoped we wouldn't have to sell right away." The sudden emotion in her chest crushed her. She was letting Daddy down. He'd been excited about producing and selling the hay, and she wouldn't be able to make it happen. Not this year, anyway. "I guess we'll have to wait on the farm equipment."

"I'm sorry. I tried everywhere."

"I know you did. Don't worry. That's life on a cattle ranch. Unpredictable." She rounded the desk, took a seat and gestured for him to also. "What else is going on?"

"Still looking for the cabin crasher." He lowered his frame into the chair opposite her desk.

"No leads?"

"No, and I've ridden back twice. No one has been there again that I can tell." He looked like he was going to say more, and she tilted her head slightly to encourage him. "I've put feelers out about it around the ranch. The only two cowboys I'm not sure of are Jake and Ryder. They're young."

"Youth isn't a crime."

"No, but I know the type."

"Do you? From personal experience?" She couldn't imagine straitlaced Clint as a troublemaker.

"I guess you could say that."

"Were you trouble with a capital *T*?" she teased.

"My grandfather thought so."

"But you only lived with him as a small child, right? Or did I remember that wrong?"

"Until I was six. I'm sure I was a pest."

"You, a pest?" She propped her elbows on the desk and rested her chin on her fist. Thinking about him as a child made her worries disappear. She tried to picture him as a little boy. "No way. I'm guessing you were adorable with those big blue eyes. You must have been a quiet kid."

"Um, I guess." He ran his fingers through his hair. "What about you? I don't see you as being quiet."

She chuckled. "I wasn't quiet, but I was very girlie."

"I'm not surprised."

"I wore dresses and pretended I was a princess. My mom and I had tea parties and baked cookies and planned special parties for my friends." She let the sweet memories seep inside. "I had a really great childhood."

The things he'd told her about his dad and grandfather came back. She suppressed a groan. She'd been insensitive. "I'm sorry. I forgot you didn't have a home like mine growing up. Do you have good memories? Who raised you after your grandfather?"

"Sure, I have good memories." The starkness in his eyes convinced her he was lying. "I had a real nice foster mom right after my grandfather died."

"Why did you end up at Yearling, then?"

"Miss Joanne got sick when I was eight, and I lived in a couple other homes after hers."

"Define a couple." A sinking feeling in her chest made her want to take back the question.

He glanced up at the ceiling, his lips twisting. "Hmm. Four, I guess."

"Four? But that would mean moving almost every year."

"Yes."

"Why so many?"

He shrugged. "Crowding. Funding. Babies. I didn't mind leaving most of them."

She rubbed her temples. "You didn't mind? But they were your families."

"No, they weren't." His dry laugh held no pleasure. "There are a lot of great foster parents out there, but besides Miss Joanne, I wouldn't call any of the people I lived with before Yearling my family. The guys I met there? They're my brothers. And Dottie and Big Bob have always looked out for me."

"How did you meet the Laverts?"

"They ran Yearling while I was there. Dottie still watches out for me. Listen, I'm not complaining. I had a roof over my head and food to eat my entire life."

"There's more to life than food and shelter."

"Miss Joanne taught me that."

"Tell me about her."

Clint shifted in his seat. "I went to live with her—she had two other foster kids, too—after my grandfather died. She taught us Bible stories and played board games with us. I was pretty broken up when she got sick and had to move back in with her folks in Idaho."

"And you said you were eight when she left? Where did you go next?"

He shrugged. "A lot of places. Some good. Some bad. None lasted."

The picture he painted sounded bleak. No mother to comfort him. No father to ride around a ranch with. No childhood home. Just random people he had no choice but to live with. She'd been fortunate to have had two parents raising her.

"We should probably discuss the sale next week," Clint said, clearly wanting to change the subject. "The vaccinations are done. Jerry and I will..." He filled her in on all the sale details, but she had a hard time concentrating. She found herself wanting to know more about the man in front of her. And wanting to give him some of his lost childhood back.

When they'd discussed the sale and other items on the agenda, Clint stood to leave.

"I've been meaning to ask—how is Banjo?" Lexi followed him out of her office through the hall.

"Fine. I've been letting him sleep on my floor at night. He won't take no for an answer."

"You're a good man, Clint." They stopped in the living room.

He looked ready to argue. With a glance at the far wall and the fireplace, he shifted his jaw. "Don't start a fire in the fireplace until I get a chance to inspect it. I'll get to it after we sell the calves."

A good man? If she only knew the memories she'd kicked up with her innocent questions, she wouldn't be so quick to brand him. Unexpected emotion had hit him hard in her office, and at first he couldn't define the feeling. But then he'd realized it was sadness. Long ago he'd stopped hoping to experience the things she described. He'd never known his mother or had the sense of belonging to parents the way most kids did. How many times had adults given up on him? How many adults had he given up on?

Lord, I know who I am. Lexi acts as if we're from the same world, but we aren't. I want to live up to her expectations, but I'm not going to fool myself into thinking I can.

Clint trudged through the snow on his way to the ranch office. He was her employee. Nothing more. And now that he had her approval, he could call the auction house and confirm next Wednesday's sale date.

As he strode past outbuildings, he saw someone duck into the horse barn. Logan? No, Logan had told him earlier he was checking calves. Clint detoured to the barn, his eyes adjusting to the dimmer light, his nose trained to smell anything beyond manure and hay. Nothing seemed out of the ordinary. He inspected the empty stalls as he walked past them then heard rustling in a stall in the opposite aisle.

"Who's there?"

Jake's head appeared, and he held a pitchfork in one hand. His face was flushed. The kid had *guilty* written all over him. "Just cleaning out stalls, boss."

"It's Thursday. You're supposed to be in school." Jake and Ryder were seniors in high school and only came in on weekends or in the afternoon during the occasional busy times throughout the year.

"I don't have class right now."

Somehow Clint doubted it. He made his way over to the stall Jake was supposedly cleaning out. "So you decided to muck stalls between classes?"

"Yep." Jake's brown eyes darkened. He wore old jeans, a stained work coat and gloves. A stocking cap covered his overgrown brown hair. With the exception of not wearing his winter overalls, the kid was dressed to work, but Clint wasn't buying his story.

"Didn't see your car out front. How'd you get here?"

"A buddy dropped me off." He shifted as if to block Clint's view of the straw bales behind him.

"Hmm." He tried to see around Jake without being obvious. "How are you getting back to school?"

"He'll pick me up later." Jake wrapped both hands around the pitchfork and leaned on it.

Whatever he was up to, it wasn't cleaning horse stalls. A dozen possibilities came to mind. He could have run away from home for a day or two. Maybe he'd stashed a bag with some clothes behind the straw. Or the kid could be playing hooky for whatever reason.

He should command Jake to move out of the way, but compassion stopped him. Clint had told Lexi the condensed version of his years in foster care. What he hadn't told her was the abusive foster home he'd been assigned to right after he turned thirteen. He'd stuck it out for a month, but the family's eighteen-year-old son kept using him as a punching bag. Clint had called his caseworker. A week later she still hadn't come out to visit, so he ran away, staying with a school buddy for a night or two then moving to another friend's house. When he'd overstayed his welcome, he contacted his caseworker again, and she told him to return to the foster family until she found him a new place.

He'd refused.

She'd tried to get him to tell her where he was staying, but he knew she'd just take him back. She asked him to call her the following week while she worked on finding a new home for him. He didn't tell her he'd been hiding out in a barn. The weather had been mild that June, and the situation suited him fine. A couple jars of peanut butter and cheap bread kept the hunger pains at bay. True to her promise, his caseworker had secured him a spot at the Yearling Group Home, and he'd moved in the following week.

Those two weeks in the barn had changed him,

though. And if Jake was dealing with similar issues, Clint wanted to help.

"How are things at home?" Clint leaned against the wood post, crossing one foot over the other.

"Fine. Why wouldn't they be?"

"I don't know. You live with your folks?"

"My dad and stepmom." His shoulders braced defiantly.

"Do you get along with them okay?"

Jake averted his eyes. "I guess."

"If something's going on—"

"Nothing's going on. I just came in to work. That's all."

Clint regarded him a moment and decided to drop the subject. "Call your buddy and have him pick you up now. We'll see you Saturday morning." He turned to leave.

"Whatever, dude," he muttered.

"What did you say?" Clint pivoted back. This kid was really pushing it with him.

"Nothing." He propped the pitchfork against the stall and pulled out an old cell phone from his pocket.

Clint began walking away, then paused. "Oh, and from now on, I don't expect to see you here unless it's your scheduled shift. Got it?"

Jake nodded before texting his friend.

Out in the fresh air once more, Clint's cell phone rang. He wanted to ignore it, but maybe it was the Montana ranch with news about selling him feed.

He answered, not slowing his pace.

"How is life working on a ranch again, man?"

Clint grinned. Nash Bolton was one of his best friends from his days at Yearling. It had been a while since they'd talked. Clint hadn't been specific about where he was working, because Nash had left Sweet Dreams under mysterious circumstances. Clint wasn't sure how he'd react to him being back.

"It's good." He checked his watch. Lunchtime. He needed a break. He could inspect the stall Jake had been in later. Changing course, he headed back to his cabin. "How are you? Haven't seen your name in the papers lately."

"Yeah, got bucked hard two weeks ago. Broke a couple ribs and my ankle. I'm mending fine." Nash had risen to bull-riding stardom right after high school. He'd won the Professional Bull Riders world championship seven years ago, and he still competed on the circuit despite the never-ending injuries plaguing him. "I've been off my feet, and I couldn't be more bored. Figured it was time for you, Wade, Marshall and me to plan a get-together. Haven't seen you since, what, September?"

"Yeah, September sounds about right. Where are you staying?"

"I'm holed up in one of Wade's empty cabins. He remodeled them all. Must have sunk a lot of cash into them, too, because I'm telling you what, I'm living in style. I'll hate to leave this luxury next month."

Their friend Wade Croft owned property all over the state, but his ranch was only a thirty-minute drive from Sweet Dreams. With Nash staying at Wade's, Clint had even more incentive to visit soon.

"Another month, huh? What next?"

"Doc wants me to retire."

Clint stopped in his tracks. Nash had never talked about retiring. Every season it was broken bones, sprains and bruises, but he kept on riding, laughing off any suggestion of quitting. "Are your injuries more serious than you're letting on?"

"No, of course, not. The wear and tear is getting to me. Maybe I'll come visit you before I decide."

"Yeah, about that… The ranch isn't in Cheyenne. I moved back to Sweet Dreams. Rock Step Ranch. I'm working for Lexi—Alexandra Harrington." His cabin came into view, and he loped the rest of the way.

"What? Why didn't you tell me?" Nash sounded angry.

"I didn't know if it would work out."

"Why wouldn't it work out?"

Clint hadn't told anyone all the details of losing his property. He'd simply told them he made a mistake and lost it. While Marshall accepted his words at face value, Wade and Nash had pressed for the full story. Regardless, Clint had remained silent. Wade and Nash had both become successful beyond any of their wildest dreams, and Clint didn't want them thinking less of him. He also knew they would have offered him money. Money he never dared take. He couldn't think of anything sadder than borrowing from them and losing their cash, too.

"Have you seen… Never mind."

Clint knew exactly whom Nash was referring to. Amy Deerson. "In church. In passing. Lexi's friends with her." He let himself into the cabin, peeling off a layer of outerwear in the process. "I should have told you this was where I was working. Dottie was the one who convinced me to try it."

"How is Dottie? I haven't seen her in years. And don't apologize—I'm glad you finally realized you were meant to work on a ranch. The job with the oil company was killing you."

"It feels good spending my day in the saddle again."

"Boy, don't I know that. When are you free? You should come up to Wade's. I'll call Marshall. It's past time we got together."

"Call Marshall and get back to me. I can't get away next week, but after that I'll find time to drive up."

"Will do. I miss you. Talk to you later." He hung up.

Clint tossed the phone on the table and stalked to the fridge. What was going on? Nash never said things like *I miss you*. First he'd mentioned retiring, and then he said he missed him? Maybe the bull had tossed him on his head.

The day they met flashed in Clint's mind. Nash had been sitting on one of the top bunks in the room they shared with Marshall and Wade. His legs dangled over the edge of the mattress, his feet in dirty athletic shoes with a hole in one toe. Nash had taken one look at Clint and said, "You got a problem with the bottom bunk?"

Clint had tossed his bag on the floor and replied, "No. Do you?"

And Nash's million-dollar smile had spread across his face. He'd hopped off the bunk, stood in front of Clint and grinned. "We're going to be good friends, you and I."

Clint had never had anyone accept him like that. And Nash had been right. They were good friends. The closest thing to a family he had.

He had a good life here. He had enough. So why couldn't he stop wanting more?

"Thank you for calling me back, Dr. Lotusmeyer. I have some questions regarding my father's health." Lexi twirled a pen between her fingers. Since Clint left, she'd spent her time trying different napkin and flatware options until choosing three potential combinations for the wedding she was planning for June. She'd taken pictures and emailed them to her assistant, Jolene, for feedback right as the doctor called.

"I'm sorry about your loss, Ms. Harrington."

"Thank you. Unfortunately, my father's death came as a complete surprise to me. He hadn't told me about his cancer diagnosis, and until recently, I assumed he hadn't known, either. But I found his pathology report. It's dated back in October. Is it normal to go from diagnosis to… well…death in such a short period of time?"

"Cancer isn't always predictable. Some people go into remission for years."

Had her father been in remission for years and she hadn't known about that, either?

"Was this the first time he'd been diagnosed with cancer?" She held her breath, not knowing what she wanted to hear, just certain the doctor could make this gnawing question mark in her heart go away.

"Yes, this was the first time he was diagnosed. It's important you mention your father's disease to your primary physician so he or she can make sure you get the recommended health screenings."

A surge of relief rushed through her body at hearing this was his first diagnosis, but the information brought new questions.

"Are you saying this could have been prevented?"

"Not at all. But early treatment can make a big difference."

"Treatment. Like chemotherapy and radiation."

"Yes. But they don't always work. Some patients die while being treated. Other patients live for years without treatment. It depends on the type of cancer and the overall health of the individual."

She really wanted to know one thing. "Was my father open to getting treatment?"

"I can't answer that."

She closed her eyes, tightening her grip around the pen. How hard could it be for him to give her a simple yes or no?

He continued. "I can tell you he had a follow-up appointment scheduled for the day after he died. I would have discussed his treatment options at that time."

Hope unfurled her fingers, and the pen fell to the desk. "Thank you for telling me. It… It's a relief."

"It's difficult losing someone suddenly. You'll have to excuse me, but I have an appointment. You take care, and have a Merry Christmas."

"Thank you. Same to you."

She hung up the phone and padded out of the office to the living room. Standing before the large windows, she took in the view of the winter countryside and shivered. Her father hadn't known about the cancer for long, and he'd made the follow-up appointment. That had to mean something, right?

She curled her fingers around her forearms, barely noticing the softness of the cashmere sweater. Maybe he'd planned on getting treatment.

Maybe he had planned on telling her. In his own time.

She'd never know.

She wished he would have trusted her enough to tell her right away.

Lord, I'm trying to get some closure. I don't know how. Everyone dies. I know it. But I'm struggling with all these questions. What do I do?

The Bible on the mantel caught her eye. She took it from its spot, caressing the hard cover. Daddy had told her to read a psalm when life got tough. She flipped through, skimming until she landed on Psalm 119:76. "May Your unfailing love be my comfort, according to Your promise to Your servant."

Unfailing love?

How many times had she skipped church, failed to pray, relied on herself, ignored the needs of those around her and brushed her own dad off? Too many to count.

She dropped onto the couch as regret and shame flowed thicker than sludge through her veins. *Lord, I'm sorry. I always put myself first.*

Visions of the weddings she planned flitted to her mind. Decorating Clint's Christmas tree did, too. Okay, she didn't *always* put herself first. But her motives were still selfish. She liked planning weddings and made a very good income at it. And the Christmas tree was more about having fun with Clint than anything else.

Lord, can You really love me with an unfailing love? I don't deserve it. Well, I guess no one does. That's the whole reason why You came down, lived a perfect life, died and rose again. Why do I conveniently forget that part?

Maybe she didn't need all the answers to move forward. She couldn't change the past, but she could pray about the future.

Chapter Seven

"Do you want Logan to go with you?"

At Lexi's innocent question, Clint pressed the accelerator. The wind was picking up, but the roads weren't icy. They'd make it to church early, so there was no reason for him to speed up. He was just frustrated. He eased his boot from the gas pedal to slow down.

"No, with Jerry sick, I need Logan to stay and take care of the remaining herd." Why had Jerry come down with pneumonia at this critical time? Clint dreaded not having the older man's expertise at the auction. Decisions would have to be made. He didn't want the responsibility of making them.

"Do you want me to come with you?"

Yes. He glanced over at her. "I thought you had a call with the senator."

"The senator's daughter." Her light brown eyes couldn't hide the truth from him. She needed to take the call. "I don't normally cancel, but if it would help, I'll reschedule."

"No need. I've got this. I've researched current prices. I'll check again tomorrow to see if they change, and I'll print them out for you to review. I'm not going to sugarcoat it—prices are low."

Being responsible for the ranch's future weighed on his shoulders, reminded him of his past.

"I know. We'll manage."

The white church came into view. He wished he shared Lexi's faith that they'd manage, but he had a lot of doubts. It cost a large amount of money to run an operation the size of Rock Step Ranch, and no matter how many times he added the numbers, the bottom line looked inadequate.

He turned into the parking lot, found a spot and cut the engine. "What if the calves don't bring enough in to cover expenses?"

"The ranch has reserves, and I have a nest egg, Clint. I'll use both if I have to."

His mind blanked.

A nest egg.

He'd lost one once. He could not be responsible for losing hers, too. How could she trust him like this with her future?

Clenching his jaw, he knew what he had to do. He had to come clean and warn her that she was putting her faith in the wrong guy.

"Lexi, I have to tell you something."

"What is it?"

"I owned property a while back. Almost five years ago. And I made a bad decision and lost it."

She scooted closer and touched his hand. "I wondered about the time between jobs."

"I don't know if I'm the best person to make these financial decisions."

"But you don't." Her voice was soothing. "I make them."

"Yes, but—"

"Look, whatever happened is in the past. Ranching is a tough business, especially for anyone just starting out. I trust you."

The words gripped him, made him want to believe she had reason to trust him. But she didn't know the circumstances of how he lost his land, and he debated telling her the rest. There were three things he'd never told a living soul. One was that his grandfather had called him a worthless brat every day for the two years he'd lived with him. Another was he'd cried every night for a month after Miss Joanne moved, and he'd hated his new foster family although they were nice people. And the third was he'd known better than to make a business deal with a virtual stranger, but he'd been too greedy to say no.

If he told his friends or Lexi any of these things, they'd see him in a different light. He'd once more become the worthless, lonely kid who didn't deserve a home or family. The day he'd taken his last punch from the kid at the foster home was the day he'd said goodbye to his former self. He'd promised himself he'd stop hoping for the family everyone else seemed to have. He'd accepted he was alone, and he'd set out to make a life for himself no one could take away.

But it had been taken away.

And he'd spent four years in penance, punishing himself for becoming the worthless, undeserving kid again. Maybe that was his problem. Once more he'd found something he wanted that could be taken away, and it scared him.

"Can we go in now?" Lexi asked.

Her lips were glossy, her skin smooth, and she looked more rested than when they first met. He shook away his thoughts. *You're not that kid anymore, so stop acting like it.*

"Yeah, let's go." He'd taken some of the weight off her slender shoulders. She needed him to be strong, to get the best price for the calves, and he would do that for her. Even if his best wasn't good enough.

"What is your favorite Christmas hymn?" Lexi turned slightly to face Clint after church. He was dead silent as he drove them home. The wind from earlier had grown more intense, and Lexi tried to ignore it, but the way it shook the truck made her doubly glad Clint was the one driving.

Church had been uplifting, and her mood was buoyant ever since Clint had confided in her. He hoarded personal details of his life. She had no doubt it had been difficult for him to admit he'd lost his property. She relished the fact he'd opened up to her. While she was curious about the details, she hadn't pressed. If he wanted her to know, he'd tell her in his own time.

"Christmas hymn? I don't know."

"Come on. You must like one."

"Haven't thought about it." The words were clipped. He didn't bother looking at her.

Refusing to take his curtness personally, she debated how far to push him. Now that he'd opened up a little, she wanted to know more about his past. She'd assumed he'd always been single, but he never talked about it. Maybe he'd lost his land in a divorce.

"Have you ever been married?" She held her breath, hoping he'd say no.

He shot her a horrified glance. "No."

Good. "Serious girlfriend?"

"'Away in a Manger.'"

She burst out laughing. "Okay, but what about my other question?"

"You first." His eyes gleamed with interest and… vulnerability.

"'Joy to the World.'"

"And the other question?" He returned his focus to the road.

Fair enough. If she wanted the real stuff from him, she'd have to pony it up herself.

"No to marriage, yes to serious relationship." She waited for the regret and sadness that flashed whenever thoughts of previous boyfriends came to mind, but they didn't bother her today. "I dated a few guys in college. Very serious types. One was determined to be a lawyer. I got in the way of his studies, so he broke it off. The other was in the engineering program."

"What happened with him?"

"Let's just say circuits and electrical waves interested him way more than I did. Our breakup was mutual. After I graduated, I got busy with planning weddings."

"And you didn't have time to date." His matter-of-fact tone had her shaking her head.

"I didn't say that. I met Doug. He was an accountant. We got along well. We did things like visiting the art museum and going out for brunch. We would join mutual friends for dinner. I thought he might be the one."

Clint's hands twisted around the steering wheel, and his jaw shifted.

"But you know what? I was wrong. He wasn't the one

at all. I've always wanted more, and I think I was willing to settle for less."

"Did he ask you to marry him or something?"

She'd thought she'd known Doug, but she'd put him on a pedestal. She'd assumed he wanted the same things she did—marriage, kids—but he hadn't. And worst of all, she'd overlooked the fact he didn't have a romantic bone in his body. She wanted a love like her parents had—affectionate and loyal and lasting—but she also wanted someone to sweep her off her feet.

"Not quite. We were at a restaurant. He asked me to move in with him. I told him I had no intention of living with anyone without being married. He seemed surprised, told me that a wedding would be too big of a distraction while he was working toward his CPA license. I understood. But then he grew agitated, said he really didn't see marriage in his future and claimed I only wanted his money. I threw a dinner roll at his chest. Never saw him again."

Clint's laugh was loud and unexpected. She started laughing, too, as they rumbled up the long road leading to the house.

"He was stupid." Clint parked the truck and turned to her. "Even I know a wedding planner doesn't want to just live with a guy. You deserve more."

And just like that, something changed inside her. The switch she'd been manning with an iron hand flipped, allowing her to view him as an eligible man. A dangerous thing, indeed. She couldn't fall for Clint. It would be awkward and end badly. He was her employee.

"What do you look for in a girl?"

"Nothing. I don't… I'm not looking for a relationship."

"Why? Did someone break your heart?"

"I never had a heart to break."

She pushed down her disappointment. She should be happy. He'd said the exact the words she needed to hear. She always fell for the reserved ones, ignoring the fact they were emotionally unavailable. She *did* have a heart to break. And Clint wouldn't be the one to break it, not if she kept her head on straight.

Thursday morning Clint sat on his couch, mindlessly petting Banjo, who had curled up next to him. He'd made a habit out of sitting for a while in front of the Christmas tree. He liked the peaceful feeling it gave him. After helping Logan feed the cattle this morning, he'd come back here to get his thoughts straight before his weekly meeting with Lexi. Yesterday's sale had gone as expected. Low prices.

Had he missed something? Was there anything he could have done to sell the calves for more money? After the meeting, he was going to ride out and check as many pregnant cows as possible. He would do his best to make sure next year's calves were born healthy.

He bundled up and headed to Lexi's with Banjo on his heels. For the fifteenth time this week, his conversation with Lexi on the way home from church came to mind. The fact she'd had serious boyfriends hadn't surprised him, but his reaction at hearing about them had.

He'd been jealous.

Worse, he'd gotten mad at this Doug character, and he hadn't even met him. Boy, he would have liked to have seen the look on the guy's face when Lexi beaned him with a dinner roll. He chuckled.

When she'd asked him if someone had broken his heart, he'd answered truthfully. But the more he thought about it, the more he realized it wasn't actually true. His heart had been broken, but not by a woman. By Devon Fields, the man who stole his land and money. From the time he was thirteen, Clint had only ever allowed himself to want one thing, and when it was taken from him, he'd fenced in his heart, the way he fenced in pastures. It was better for him not to want too much. For his own protection.

But Lexi… How did she do it? Give her heart out freely? Wear optimism and faith in mankind on her sleeve even when she had reasons not to? Her dad's betrayal could have shut her down, made her paranoid and petty. The ex-boyfriends could have made her doubt love.

Somehow, he knew she still was open to love.

And she should be. She should have a wedding with pink silk and gobs of flowers and fancy tables and whatever else she put together for all those other couples.

He reached the path to her house. "Banjo, go to the barn." He pointed to the barn, and Banjo loped away.

Two minutes later Clint approached Lexi's office. The room was more girlie than it had ever been, and that was saying something. Weird netting stuff was draped over the bookcases. A table had been set up with a white tablecloth, fine china, silverware, fancy glasses, note cards and a vase full of light pink flowers. Lexi's back was to him, and she was tucking a black ribbon in place. She stood back, surveyed the bow, and nudged it a fraction. Her hair was pulled back in a low ponytail, and she wore a dark purple sweater over tight black pants.

"What do you think?" She tapped her chin.

You're the most beautiful woman I've ever seen. He cleared his throat. "It's nice."

"Nice?" She frowned. "You don't like it?"

"I like it."

"No, you don't. It's the white tablecloth, isn't it? Ivory would be more elegant."

"Aren't white and ivory the same thing?"

"Oh, you!" She laughed, waving as if he'd made a joke. "That's good. Ivory and white. The same." Still chuckling, she sat at her desk.

He wasn't sure why she was laughing, but he dropped into the chair opposite her and slid the folder with the sale papers her way. "Here's all the documentation from the sale."

She skimmed the top sheet, licked her finger and flipped to the next one, perusing each until closing the folder and setting it down.

"I know I've expected a lot from you and you haven't been here long, but I'm really grateful for all you do. Thank you for handling the sale."

"I wish I could have gotten more money for you."

Her smile revealed white teeth. "Don't worry about it. You did your best."

His best wasn't good enough.

"Your father might have gotten more."

"I doubt it. The market is what it is. He had many years when he fretted about the sale."

Was she trying to make him feel better, or was she telling the truth? Looking in her eyes, he saw honesty. They were open, trusting. The kind of expression he wanted to live up to but doubted he could. It wasn't only his performance as ranch manager he wanted to impress her with. He wouldn't mind if she saw more in him as a man.

Averting his eyes, he felt heat climb his neck. Where had that thought come from?

He could no longer deny it.

He'd gone way beyond thinking of her as his boss.

"How did the call go yesterday?" He shifted in his seat, hoping she hadn't somehow picked up on his train of thought. He could *not* afford to let her know he was getting feelings for her or that just the thought of seeing her made his heart beat faster. Schoolboy stuff. A couple days out in frozen pastures would get him back to normal.

"It went really well. Madeline knows what she wants and asked me to send her pictures with my vision. That's why I'm staging the table. I'll have to wait until the other linens I ordered arrive to finish it." She gestured to the table. "This tablecloth won't do at all. I'm going to send three possibilities. Hopefully, she'll like one enough to get started. What else is going on?"

They discussed ranch details for the next half hour.

"I'm heading out to check all the pregnant cows." He stood. His gaze fell to her lips, and he snapped his eyes shut. *God, give me strength to walk out of here and get her off my mind.* "I'll leave you to your decorating."

She strolled next to him down the hallway. "I don't mean to be a pain, but I've been thinking it's not the Christmas season without a fire in the fireplace."

An excuse to see her again. Soon. Adrenaline rushed through his veins. Even though he knew it wasn't smart, he said, "I'll come by Saturday afternoon and check your fireplace. But you have to promise me you won't start a fire before then."

She smiled, biting her lower lip. That did it. He had to get out of here before he did something really stupid, like tell her she looked like a cowboy's dream in that cute little sweater of hers.

Chapter Eight

"Come on in!" Lexi opened the door wide and ushered Clint inside late Saturday afternoon. The sky was already growing dark and it was only four o'clock. A gentle snow had been falling for the past hour. All morning she'd cleaned the house, ridiculously excited not to be alone on another Saturday night. And while spending it with Clint wasn't the wisest choice, she'd prayed about it and was reasonably confident she could keep her feelings under control if she reminded herself they could only be friends.

Clint set his tool belt on the floor and shrugged out of his coat and boots. His gray T-shirt left nothing to the imagination where his muscles were concerned, and his dark jeans fit him just right. *He works for you. And he's not looking for a relationship.* She forced herself to return to the living room.

Her Christmas tree sparkled with white lights, purple and silver ornaments, and violet garland winding around the tree. Daddy would have liked this one. He would have teased her and called it the lilac tree. Lately she'd been able to think about him without wanting to cry.

"See you Saturday," he said gruffly. Then he gave her a nod and hurried out the door.

Only when he was striding to the stables did he begin to breathe normally again. What was wrong with him? Thinking of Lexi as a woman? He knew better. If he didn't rein these feelings in, he would lose his job. This ranch wasn't his, but it was all he had. Without it, he didn't know what he would do.

Clint entered and knelt by the fireplace.

She put her hand on her hip. "I hope you like pizza."

He opened the glass doors and poked his head under the fireplace opening.

"Do I take your silence to mean you don't like pizza?" She moved closer to the hearth.

He sat up, his sheepish smile making her chest flutter. Clint smiling brought his attractiveness to a whole new level. "I like pizza."

"Good. Because I bought one from the Pizza Factory earlier. I figure we can heat it up later."

"That would be fine. I hope I didn't bother you this morning. I went up on the roof to inspect the chimney. The chimney cap is in good shape. I'm guessing your father had it replaced recently."

"I wouldn't know." For several years, she really hadn't known what Daddy was doing on a daily basis. When they would talk on the phone, they'd catch up on ranch news, the weddings she was planning and things like that. Mundane items hadn't been discussed. And for once, she kind of wished they'd talked about it all. What else had she missed while she was building her empire in Denver?

"I'll give this a look." He beamed the flashlight around and slid a lever back and forth. Then he moved the light across the entire interior of the fireplace. "The damper is working fine. I don't see any signs of moisture or cracking in here, either. I think you're okay. Let me grab some wood and newspaper, and I'll get a fire started to make sure it's safe."

He left the room. The inspection had taken all of ten minutes. Knowing Clint, he'd find an excuse to leave as soon as the fire got going and they'd eaten. And she'd be alone. As usual.

She'd assumed he'd want to hang out with her. Maybe she'd been wrong. Couldn't hurt to ask. He'd fight her—he usually did—but she wanted him to stay.

Holding an armful of logs, he came back into the room. "I'll be right back with newspaper. Do you have matches?"

"I do." She went to the kitchen and searched the junk drawer until she found a box. Taking her time, she returned to the living room and held the box out to Clint. "Are you busy tonight?"

"No, why?"

"I was going to watch a Christmas movie after dinner. You're welcome to stay."

He took the box, his fingers brushing hers, and his eyes darkened, gleaming. "Okay."

Okay? Just like that? "I mean, you don't have to, but I… Well, it's been kind of lonely here, and I wouldn't mind the company."

"Yeah. I'll stay." His matter-of-fact tone surprised her. He wasn't one to answer quickly. And he usually had to be convinced. What was going on with him?

"Are you sure?" She crossed her arms over her chest.

"I wouldn't mind watching a movie." He began to stack the wood inside the fireplace. Then he tucked wadded newspaper rolls underneath the logs. "Come here a minute."

Her pulse took off. Why did he want her over there? She bent next to him, inhaling the clean scent of soap and aftershave on his skin.

Maybe she shouldn't have asked him to stay. His nearness gave her a jittery sensation.

"See this hook?" He pointed to the lever inside the fireplace.

"Yes."

"It's the damper. Move it like this to open it before you start a fire. If it's not open, smoke will fill the house." He took her hand and moved the damper with it. His fingers were warm, strong. She could feel his breath on her cheek.

She didn't blink. Didn't move. If she did she feared she'd turn her head and…

"Why don't I heat up the pizza?" She stood abruptly and backed up two steps.

"And I'll get the fire started." His voice sounded coarse.

They didn't need a fire. Ten seconds near Clint and she was warmer than she'd thought possible. As she made her way to the kitchen, she mentally kicked herself. She was too attracted to him.

No, she was lonely. That was it. This empty Wyoming land combined with the big house and no daily interaction with her Denver employees had warped her. Made her desperate for company.

She turned on the oven. Who was she kidding? The days she'd spent in Denver last week had been just as lonely, just as desperate.

Ever since Daddy died, an unwelcome solitude had descended that she couldn't shake.

After popping the pizza into the oven, she set the timer and joined Clint in the living room. A small fire had come to life, and he was inspecting one of the spots where a stone was missing.

"I see rocks like these near the river all the time. If you'd like, I'll try to find some to fit these empty spaces."

"That would be great. The fireplace was built with stones found on the property." She sat on the couch, tucking her legs under her bottom. "Clint?"

"Hmm?" He stuck a screwdriver into the mortar.

"You've been an orphan a long time."

"Yeah."

"Do you ever feel lonely? Like you don't belong anywhere in the world?"

He faced her, his expression serious. "Lonely? Sure, sometimes. Like I don't belong? Always."

That's what she'd been afraid of. She pressed her palms to her cheeks and whispered, "I'm scared."

He put the screwdriver down and joined her on the couch. Sitting next to her, he reached to take her hand. "You don't have to be scared, Lexi. It was different for me. I never had a place like this. A home. You belong here. You'll always belong here."

"But I feel displaced without my father." She fought the emotion tightening her throat. "I took him for granted. I didn't come home enough. I didn't—"

Clint wrapped his arm around her shoulders, and she leaned her cheek against his chest. She could feel his heartbeat through his shirt.

"Don't," he said softly. "Don't do this to yourself."

"I can't help it." Her voice sounded small. "I was so busy, so happy, so selfish. All the time working on my business, planning the weddings—I didn't see… And now I can't."

"That's not true. You're not selfish." His hand caressed her upper arm in soothing circles. "You told me yourself when you came home you always rode the property with your dad."

"But I should have done it more often. What if I'm being punished?"

He brought his arm back, turning his head to stare at her, his blue eyes shining with compassion. "For what?"

"For wanting too much."

"We all want too much." He leaned forward, his elbows resting on knees. "You aren't being punished. You deserve good things."

The timer went off, startling her. She had to get herself together. What was her problem, anyway? One minute she was asking him to stay for a movie, and the next she revealed her deepest fears?

And what in the world happened to her decision to keep their relationship professional? Hadn't she warned herself to be careful? Lonely or not, she had a lot to lose if Clint quit.

She'd lose her manager, but worse, she'd lose his friendship.

Are you really trying to tell yourself he's just a friend?

The smell of oregano and mozzarella reminded her the pizza was probably burning. She hurried to the kitchen. After taking the pizza out, she brought two plates with slices to the living room. "Okay, I promise I won't be weird anymore. What movie should we watch? *Elf* or *It's a Wonderful Life*?"

"Elf."

She kept her promise. Didn't act weird or sappy or reveal any more secrets the rest of the evening. Instead, she found herself watching Clint's reaction to the movie, memorizing the way his lips curved when he laughed. Telling herself she'd go back to all business tomorrow, but tonight she'd enjoy sitting by him in front of a cozy fire with her pretty Christmas tree twinkling nearby.

Tomorrow, she'd be his boss. Tonight, she'd enjoy his company.

The following morning, Clint shifted in his seat next to Lexi at church. The pastor was midway through the sermon, but no matter how hard Clint tried, he couldn't process a word the preacher said. Last night had surprised him. He'd taken one look at Lexi's fuzzy red sweater and her big eyes, and he'd agreed to pizza and a movie without putting up a fight.

Because he didn't want to fight it.

But he had to.

Had to.

He felt like an insect being spun in a spider's web, except Lexi wasn't the spider. His past was. And when she'd opened up about being lonely and feeling like she was being punished, he'd wanted to yell, *Yes, I get it, I understand. I've been punished my whole life for wanting too much.* But how could he? She actually deserved the things she thought she was being punished for, and he didn't. He'd been greedy, in a hurry and sloppy with his trust. Lexi would never be any of those things.

Clint sneaked a peek her way. She looked pale today, and her cheeks were drawn. He hoped she hadn't stayed up thinking about their conversation after he left. Frankly, he hoped she'd put those thoughts out of her head forever. He didn't want her beating herself up.

As soon as the service ended, he was riding out to inspect the cows. Jerry was still recovering from pneumonia, and his wife, who Jerry referred to as the missus, wouldn't let him come back to work until his cough was gone for good. Although Ryder and Jake were checking the herd this morning, Clint wanted to be sure none of the pregnant cows were acting off. The ranch was important to Lexi, and he wouldn't let anything jeopardize her home, including him. It was time to distance himself from his beautiful boss.

The congregation sang "Amazing Grace," and Clint found himself enthusiastically singing along. The lyrics went straight to his heart.

Thank You, Lord, for saving a wretch like me. Please let Lexi see she has nothing to feel guilty about. Fill her with the sense of belonging she's missing right now. And give me the good sense and fortitude to leave her alone.

The service ended, and they greeted other members on their way out. After helping Lexi into her coat, he took her arm to steady her over the icy sidewalk on the way back to his truck.

She didn't say a word the entire time. Unusual for her.

"Something wrong?" He opened the passenger door and boosted her up.

She shook her head.

He started the truck, knowing he should drive home and check the cows, but his conscience poked at him.

"Want to get some breakfast?" As soon as the words were out of his mouth, he held his breath, wanting her to say no. Hoping she'd say yes.

"I could eat."

"Dottie's Diner?"

"Sure."

Now why had he gone and done that? He'd told himself he needed to stay away from her. Hard to do if he kept finding excuses to prolong being near. He drove the short distance to the restaurant, and they stood inside the breezeway for several minutes as they waited for a table.

Finally, a booth opened, and Dottie stopped by with coffee as soon as they'd settled in.

"Lexi, so good to see you, sugar. How are you doing? You getting enough to eat?"

"I'm good, Dottie. Thank you for the casseroles you dropped off after the funeral. They were delicious."

"My pleasure, hon. We all loved RJ. He was a good man. And he was right proud of you, sugar. If you need anything, say the word." She turned to Clint, her face all sunshine. "I sure love having you back in Sweet Dreams, tiger."

"I like being back." It was true. He'd moved two hours away after high school and hadn't lived here in over a decade, but it was the closest thing to home he had. He didn't even mind that Dottie called him tiger.

Maybe he did belong somewhere. Sweet Dreams had been good to him.

"What can I get you two?" She untucked a pen from behind her ear and flipped a sheet on her small notepad. After Lexi ordered the Sunrise Special, he asked for the same, ignoring Dottie's wink before she left. The diner was crowded and loud and put him in a good mood.

"I didn't know you went by tiger." Lexi's eyes twinkled.

He knew his cheeks were flaming. "You're not one to talk, sugar."

She laughed. "I guess not. I know Dottie treats everyone like family, but she clearly has a soft spot for you. When you were at Yearling, did you live with them?"

"No, we lived in a bunkhouse on the ranch with a

youth care worker, and the Laverts had a small house next to us."

She twirled a straw in her glass of water. "Why were you sent there?"

He took a drink of coffee before answering. "Yearling was different than many group foster homes. They only accepted teen boys who had no chance of being placed with their parents. In my case, my parents were dead, but the other guys had parents who were abusive, addicted or imprisoned, and it limited their foster options. As long as we followed the rules—and there were many—we lived there until we aged out."

"Aged out? What does that mean?"

"When I turned eighteen, I legally had to leave the foster home because I was an adult."

"That's awful." Wrinkles appeared in her forehead. "I couldn't have lived on my own at eighteen. I was still in high school."

"So was I."

The way she stilled and stared at him made him squirm. Guffaws came from the booth behind him, and the smell of bacon filled the air. He hoped Dottie would bring their breakfasts soon so he could avoid talking about his childhood anymore.

"What in the world did you do?" She leaned in, lowering her voice. "Where did you go?"

Looked like the childhood conversation wasn't over yet.

"Big Bob helped me get hired at LFR Ranch. The Laverts always looked out for us as best they could."

"But isn't LFR Ranch a couple of hours away?" She wrapped her hands around her mug.

"I was still able to graduate. My guidance counselor

helped me the two months I was gone. I was blessed. A lot of kids have nowhere to go. They're literally homeless."

"Oh, my, I had no idea."

"Eat up, kids." Dottie placed two steaming platters of eggs, bacon, hash browns and toast in front of them. "I'll be back in a flash with more coffee."

He dug into his eggs. As much as he'd missed living with Miss Joanne, he'd been fortunate to end up at Yearling. Throughout high school he'd been in a stable environment instead of on edge about possibly being moved to another home. The one thing he'd really feared was getting kicked out, so he'd followed the rules and never bent them. Plus, he'd learned the cowboy life and gotten his first taste of ranching.

"Big Bob taught me to ride." He shook salt and pepper on his hash browns. "We all had ranch chores. I loved it. God was looking out for me there."

Lexi bit into her toast, a thoughtful expression on her face. "I guess it's all how we look at things, isn't it?"

"What do you mean?"

"You see your placement there as God looking out for you, and all I can do is feel sad that you didn't grow up under the care of your parents."

"I try not to think about it. Doesn't change things." He used to think about it. A lot. He'd wanted Miss Joanne to be his mom. He'd resented the homes he'd been shuffled to. In the deepest part of him, he'd wondered what was wrong with him. Why was he worthless? Why did no one ever even come close to wanting to adopt him? Why didn't he have parents? As the years progressed, he'd come to terms with the fact he wasn't meant to be part of a loving family.

"Well, at least when you have babies, you'll be able to give them all the things you missed." She sipped her coffee before taking another bite of bacon.

Babies? He'd never thought about having babies. Sure, he liked kids, but families were for other people. Weren't they?

His chest tightened, and he was finding it hard to breathe. *Great.* The thought of kids was giving him a heart attack.

"I have to admit," she said. "I thought I'd be married and starting a family by now."

He could easily see her holding a baby or two. "You'll be a great mother."

Her face fell. "Well, it's kind of a moot point. I'm not starting the family until I get married." She raised her left hand and pointed to the ring finger. "And it hasn't happened yet. I'm not sure it ever will."

"Any single guy in this town would drop to a knee and propose in a minute." As the words left his mouth, the tightness in his chest amplified. Why would he tell her that? It was true, but he didn't want a bunch of guys sniffing around the ranch to date her.

She shook her head, a big smile on her face. "Oh, Clint, you crack me up. No one in Sweet Dreams is beating down the door to date me."

Yet. Frowning, he attacked the food on his plate. He didn't see what was so funny. He'd spoken the truth. If any of these guys thought they had even the slimmest of chances with her, they'd be wooing her.

Wooing? Now he sounded like Jerry with his old-timer sayings. And anyhow, it wasn't any of Clint's business if someone wanted to date Lexi or if she got married. He was only there to do a job.

And what would happen when she did get married? Any guy in his right mind would want to run Rock Step Ranch. Clint wouldn't be needed there anymore. Or if she married someone without ranch experience, Clint would have to take orders from him.

He lost his appetite.

"Can we walk around town a little after breakfast? I'd like to see the storefront decorations. I usually stroll around downtown Denver to get in the Christmas spirit, but this year..." She shrugged.

The cows needed to be checked, but they would have to wait. If he didn't walk her around town, someone else might, and he wasn't ready to think about getting another job or worry about her getting married. The bottom line? He couldn't afford a heart attack this close to Christmas. Guess he was strolling around Sweet Dreams.

What had possessed her to talk about babies with Clint? Lexi huddled under her scarf as she strolled next to him along Main Street. One minute they'd been talking about his childhood—which was about as depressing as it could get—and the next she'd tried to make the situation better by telling him he'd be a good dad. But the whole thing had backfired. As soon as she'd mentioned babies, she'd pictured him holding one.

And Clint was gorgeous enough without adding an adorable baby to the mix.

"Well, the wind isn't so crazy now." She stopped in front of the window of the secondhand shop. Plush stuffed penguins were sitting on nests made of white lights, and children's books with penguins were propped up next to them. The longing in her heart surprised her. She hadn't thought about having babies in a long time.

Her company *was* her baby. But it felt more like a rebellious teenager lately, and she couldn't snuggle it in her arms or sing lullabies to it.

"Isn't that a cute display?" Would she ever buy little books and stuffed animals for her own children for Christmas? Life hadn't turned out the way she'd dreamed it would. What if she never got married? Never had babies to cradle in her arms?

"Uh-huh." Clint barely glanced at the window. Not a shock where he was concerned.

She'd been around him too much, and she was forgetting the things that were important to her. Maybe she was destined to be single the rest of her life. She wanted more than mutual affection, more than discussing ranch operations, more than a pleasant afternoon together.

She wanted love.

Love was intense, unpredictable. It was knowing each other's secrets. She'd seen it firsthand with friends in Denver. Her own parents had been affectionate, with eyes only for each other. She wanted the same.

"Do you want to turn around?" Her mood had slipped to melancholy. What was the point in window shopping with someone if they weren't into it?

"Whatever you want."

She almost rolled her eyes. She wanted… It didn't matter. What had Clint said at breakfast when she'd been sad he didn't have parents? *Doesn't change things.* He was right. She could want love and marriage and babies, but it didn't change things.

She needed clarity. Because living between her two worlds was getting too hard. Either she moved back to Denver and fixed her company, or she lived here permanently. She didn't see how she could continue to live here and effectively run Weddings by Alexandra. But what about her feelings for Clint?

"Let's keep going," she said brusquely. "There's not much left to see."

They passed a barber shop and a real estate agent's office with a wreath on the door and red lights shaped like cowboy boots in the window. At the end of the block, she prepared to go back, but the corner building across the street caught her eye.

"Why is the old chamber of commerce building all boarded up?" She started forward, but Clint caught her arm. Just then a vehicle turned directly in front of them.

"Whoa, there." He kept hold of her arm. "Didn't you see that truck?"

"No, I— Come on!" She checked for traffic this time and ran across the street, gazing up at the two-story brick building. It had been there forever, but she'd never paid it much attention. It had housed several businesses over the years, but the only one she could remember was the chamber of commerce, and she'd never been inside. "I wonder why it's empty. I can't believe I never really noticed it before. Whatever it was originally used for must have been important for them to put all this architectural detail into it."

Clint walked to the front, where plywood covered the large picture windows and a faded For Sale sign hung lopsided from the door. "Looks like it was a department store."

"How can you tell?"

He pointed to the bricks above the window. Engraved stones of a lighter shade spelled out Department Store.

She tossed her head back and laughed. A grin spread across his face.

The recessed entry held an old-fashioned door with peeling black paint. It had a narrow window near the top, and, standing on her tiptoes, she rubbed the dirt off with a tissue and tried to peek inside. It was hard to tell from her view, but it appeared to be a large empty space.

Perfect for a wedding reception.

"I wonder how long it's been boarded up."

He shoved his hands into his coat pockets. "Why are you excited about this place? Looks like it hasn't been used in years."

A ticker tape of things to research spun through her mind, and she craned her neck to try to see more of the interior.

"You're taller than me." She pulled him next to her and practically shoved him to the narrow window. "Can you look in there and tell me what you see?"

He peered into it. "A counter. Looks like some left-over scaffolding. I think there's a staircase."

"Is it wooden?"

He shaded his eyes to see better. "I can't tell."

"Boost me up."

"What?" With a deer-caught-in-headlights expression, he pressed his back to the alcove wall. She popped her fist on her hip and gave him her most withering glare.

"I need to know if it has hardwood floors and how the space flows."

"I'll check again."

"I won't be able to see it through your eyes."

He exhaled. Loudly. "Fine."

"Crouch down a little. I'll step onto your thigh." She couldn't wait to see what the room looked like. Clint obeyed, and as she put her foot above his knee he hoisted her up, his hands around her waist. Even through her wool coat, she was aware of his touch.

She gasped. "It's better than I imagined! I can't really see the floors, but I can tell they're hardwood. And there *is* a staircase—I think it's original. Oh! This is the right size."

She slid down with his arms still at her waist, and spun to face him.

"The right size for what?" His voice was husky.

"A wedding reception."

The words hovered above them like the Christmas lights strung across the town, and as she met Clint's eyes, she forgot the ticker tape of things to research. Forgot the hardwood floors and breathtaking staircase. Forgot everything.

He leaned in, his blue eyes as bright as she'd ever seen them. Was he going to kiss her?

At the last second, he brushed her cheek with his lips. At his simple touch, she melted into his arms. All the burdens and guilt and worries she'd been carrying for the past two months no longer mattered. For the first time since burying her father, she belonged somewhere. In his embrace.

She didn't have to be the boss of anything—not her company, not the ranch—not with his arms locked around her and her cheek pressed against his shoulder.

Please don't let this moment end.

Clint stepped back and rubbed his neck, not looking at her.

"Don't say anything." She blinked, shaking her head. "Don't say a word. Just...thank you."

"Lexi—"

"Don't." She couldn't bear it if he announced this moment was a mistake or any other lame thing men came up with when they were afraid of getting in too deep. This had been too real, too precious to let anything ruin it.

"I'm going to find out about this building. It's the perfect place for wedding receptions. Think of all the themes I could do with it. And parties! I don't think there are any upscale reception halls in the area. Sweet Dreams has a VFW hall outside town, but frankly, it was always on the dumpy side. Don't brides in Wyoming deserve a special place to celebrate close to home? I think they do." She hooked her arm in his and told him all the ideas running through her head on the way back to the truck. He didn't say a word, and she tried not to read anything into his silence.

All she knew was she'd found two vital things in under thirty minutes: a sense she belonged and something that brought her joy.

She couldn't wait to get home and start researching.

Chapter Nine

What kind of a cotton-pickin' fool was he?

He'd almost kissed her. Sure, he'd brushed her cheek in the nick of time, but it had been a close call. Too close.

The cold air bit at his exposed cheeks as he rode around the pasture that afternoon checking pregnant cows. His insulated coveralls kept his body warm, but his heart had been chilled ever since Lexi thanked him.

She'd *thanked* him.

For what? For being inappropriate? Because he had been. At breakfast she'd been talking about babies, and then she'd been so over the moon about the abandoned building. When she'd uttered the words *wedding reception*, he'd taken one look at her face—sparkling and beautiful and good—and he'd lost his mind. And when she'd burrowed into his embrace with her cheek against his shoulder? He'd actually allowed himself a peek at the dreams he'd buried long ago.

He couldn't seem to put the dreams back. He hadn't simply held her. He'd kissed her cheek. Thought about kissing her lips. He'd taken their relationship beyond employer/employee, way past friendship…to risky.

He couldn't go any farther. Not where she was concerned.

His horse trotted through the frozen pasture around the grazing herd as snow fell. The air pinched Clint's lungs, made him feel alive. This—riding a horse on a winter day, checking pregnant cows, making sure their drinking water hadn't iced over—this was what he'd been made to do. The good Lord had blessed him with a love of ranching. And he was working on one of the finest ranches in Wyoming, so how could he jeopardize it by wanting more?

He was Lexi's employee, and his status wasn't going to change unless she fired him. He'd spent his entire life as no one's choice. There was something flawed inside him. It was why his dad had abandoned him, why his grandfather couldn't stand him, why none of the foster families considered making him a permanent part of their lives. Other kids had gotten adopted. Not him.

He belonged to nobody, and no one belonged to him. And that's the way it would stay.

Wishful thinking would only bring disappointment, the way it always had.

Lexi was nice to him because she was nice to everyone. She was lonely, needed a friend, and he was nearby.

And when she finds out the reason you lost your land?

She wouldn't want him around at all. She'd made it clear she hated being lied to. And he hadn't told her the whole truth.

Lexi made people's dreams come true. It was who she was, what she did. And she deserved someone who would make her dreams come true.

Every dream he'd had, he'd found a way to mess up.

She might not know him as a worthless brat or that

Romine kid, but he did. He'd never been enough. Never would be enough for someone like her. When she got her life figured out, she'd find someone who belonged in her world. Someone with a family who would treat her like their daughter. And she'd be happy.

With a clicking sound, he urged his horse to keep moving. A snow-covered lump caught his eye. He made his way around the cattle grazing contentedly on the prairie grass and headed toward the lump, which he could now make out beyond the ridge.

A knot formed in his gut as he realized what it was. He dismounted and lowered to one knee to make sure. A cold, unmoving heifer. He checked the tag and stood so abruptly the blood rushed from his head.

No! He bent over, bracing his hands against his thighs as the heifer's death hit him. This animal had seemed fine. How had he missed the signs? Had she been off by herself? Where had he gone wrong?

Carefully, he brushed the snow off her, looking for signs of attack or trauma, but he didn't see any. He and Logan had selected this heifer to keep based on her overall health and her mama's calving record. They'd fully expected her to be a top producer in the future.

And now she was dead.

He hadn't wanted to cry in a long time, but emotion strangled his throat. He coughed to dislodge it, but the knot forming only grew bigger.

While he'd been off with Lexi, this precious animal had died.

He got back on his horse and rode hard back to the barns. After he put the horse away, he strode to Logan's cabin, dreading the conversation he was about to have.

"Hey, Clint, what are you doing here?" Logan stood back to let him inside.

"I need you to come out to the east pasture with me."

"Why? What's wrong?" Logan shoved his feet into the boots next to the door and grabbed his heavy coat off the hook. He called over his shoulder, "I'll be back later, Sarah."

As they strode toward the stable, Clint said, "It's the thirty-six yellow-tag heifer."

Logan paused and let out a sigh. "I knew I should have checked on her this morning. I noticed she looked poorly yesterday and gave her antibiotics. How is she?"

"Dead."

Logan looked stricken. "This is all my fault."

"It's not your fault. I planned on riding out after church, but I didn't come home right away."

"It's your day off. I told Jake and Ryder to keep an eye out as they rode, but I forgot about the heifer. I should have had them check the water tanks instead of me. Man, this stinks." He slapped his thigh. "I'll tell Lexi. The heifer was my responsibility, and I let her down."

"You gave her antibiotics yesterday, so there wasn't anything more you could do. I'll tell Lexi, but for now, let's get the animal back here and try to figure out what killed her. I can't have any more cattle dying, and I want to make sure this isn't something that might spread."

If Clint had any wishful hopes about a future with Lexi, this put an end to them. He'd placed his personal life ahead of the ranch, and a heifer was dead because of it.

If he didn't get his head out of the temptation Lexi presented, he'd mess up her life as much as he'd messed up his own. He would not let that happen.

* * *

"Thanks for coming with me, Amy." Lexi rubbed her hands together as they waited for Shawn Lesly, an old family friend and local real estate agent, to open the door to the empty building. Although it was late Tuesday afternoon, she'd stopped into Amy's Quilt Shop on the off chance Amy would join her. Thankfully, Amy had agreed.

"I'm glad you asked. I can't wait to see inside!"

Lexi had spent Sunday night and all day yesterday jotting ideas and researching the surrounding area for the feasibility of opening a hall for receptions and events. She'd set up the appointment with Shawn and had wanted to ask Clint to join her today, but he'd been so down when he stopped by Sunday evening to let her know the heifer died, she hadn't had the heart to drag him from the ranch. Jerry had finally been well enough to come to work yesterday, and he'd told her Clint had been out from dawn to dusk checking fences and the herd. She had a feeling he'd be doing the same today.

Shawn, a balding man with a gray mustache, let them inside. Lexi's eyes had to adjust to the dark room.

"I talked to the listing agent, Lexi. The electricity has been off for a couple of years." He opened a folder. "Water's been shut off as well to make sure the pipes don't freeze."

Amy crossed her arms and shivered. "What's the scoop behind this building, Shawn? Didn't I hear a rumor the dollar store considered buying it a while back?"

"Yes, and that was four years ago. The dollar store found it more cost-effective to rent space in the strip mall. The heating system might need to be replaced, but the plumbing and electrical have been updated."

"Why do you think it's been empty? It's a large space and full of character." Lexi touched the beautiful wood trim. She'd preserve it, the crown molding and the staircase. She envisioned the room all polished and glowing. Brides sweeping down the staircase to meet their new grooms. People lined up on either side to cheer and welcome them.

"The owner held onto it for two years. There was interest, but he wanted top dollar for it. I was his agent at the time. Then he died and a distant relative inherited it. The woman has turned down several offers since."

"Why?" Lexi bent to check out the floor. Scratched and in need of refinishing, but it appeared to be oak. "Did she give a reason?"

"Rumor has it she's a bit particular about the type of business that goes in here. Seems she had dreams of opening a tea shop."

"Hmm… I wonder what stopped her," Amy said.

"Probably the fact she's in her late eighties." Shawn took a sheet of paper out of the folder and handed it to Lexi. "Here you go. The list price, comps and square footage."

"Thank you." She scanned the sheet, raising her eyebrows at the price. "Do you think the building is worth this much?"

"No." He tapped his chin. "But the owner might work with you on the price. Why don't you look around? I'll be down here if you have any questions."

"Let's go upstairs." Amy linked arms with Lexi, and they strode to the grand staircase off to the side. "What do you think is up there?"

"Dead mice. And hopefully more gorgeous floors and space for a smaller party. It would be nice to have a dedicated area for bridal showers, Christmas parties, anniversary parties and similar events."

They climbed the stairs, and Lexi couldn't help but pause midway to take in the main floor. With some TLC, this building could be stunning. A real gem in Sweet Dreams.

"Would you really move back, Lexi? For good?" They reached the top.

The question sent swirls of uncertainty through her stomach. Clint's eyes before he kissed her cheek came to mind. If moving back for good included exploring what could happen beyond friendship with Clint, then yes, she could easily imagine moving back. But if not? She bit the corner of her bottom lip. She wasn't sure.

"I'm not making decisions right now." She turned to view the second floor, which appeared to be split into offices with a side room perfect for entertaining a large group of people. "Just looking and seeing what my options are, but so far, this building feels as if it was built just for me. It's perfect!"

Amy glanced out of the window overlooking the side street. "What will you do with your wedding business in Denver?"

"That's the problem. I don't know. My wedding planners work on commission, and they could easily branch out on their own. But right now I take care of the business issues like insurance and meeting rooms for clients and such. Plus, they have expense accounts for up-front costs. I'd hate to put any of them in financial jeopardy by closing the business." Lexi pulled a tape measure out of her purse and measured the length of the larger room. "I thought about it a lot yesterday, and if I'm serious about moving back, then I would offer to sell the business to my vice president, Natalie."

"Would she be in a position to buy it?"

Lexi straightened, the tape measure recoiling with a snap. "I don't know. But I have to make a decision one way or the other. I can't divide my time between Wyoming and Denver forever. Both the ranch and the business demand my attention."

Amy opened a cabinet built into the wall. "I'm surprised you're considering giving it all up to move back."

"The longer I'm here, the more I feel I'm ready for a new adventure. I'm taking your advice, though, and praying about it."

"I'm glad. Keep praying, and I will, too. Does this mean you're getting some closure about your dad?"

The permanent lump in her throat had dissolved at some point over the past few weeks. "I think so. Honestly, having Clint around has helped."

Amy's smile fell. "I didn't realize you were getting close to him."

"I hadn't realized it, either."

"I didn't know him well in school… I wonder…" Amy's eyebrows drew together, then she shook her head. "Never mind."

"Don't you like him?"

"I was close to one of his friends years ago, and he turned out to be unreliable."

"I'm sorry. I didn't realize. Clint is very reliable, though, so don't worry about that." Lexi strode toward the offices. "I'd like to get him something nice for Christmas. Any ideas?"

"Well, what does he like?" Amy followed her, leaning against the doorjamb of the room Lexi was inspecting.

What *did* Clint like? "Ranching and riding and cattle."

"What about something along those lines? A gift card to the Western store would let him pick out exactly what he wants."

"I could do that." She peeked into the closet and noted the electrical sockets on the walls looked modern. "But it's impersonal. After all the work he's done to take over managing the ranch, I'd like it to be a little more special."

"Hmm...wish I could help you out, but I don't know him very well."

Lexi frowned. Clint was used to spending holidays alone. He had no family. Grew up in foster homes. He'd mentioned close friends. Besides them, did anyone really know Clint? Sympathy squeezed her heart at the loneliness of his upbringing. The adult Clint seemed secure in himself but just as alone.

She thought about his cabin with the cowboy Christmas tree. And Banjo. He'd mentioned how he enjoyed training herding dogs. He lit up whenever Banjo was around. And he'd never had a dog of his own.

What if she bought him a border collie puppy? His own herding dog to train and love? But how could she find one this close to Christmas?

"Do you know anyone who breeds border collies? Or good herding dogs?"

"Of course I do. This is Sweet Dreams." Amy smiled, waving her hand. "Dan and Lola Smith are known for their purebreds. They usually have a litter in time for Christmas, but they might all be sold."

"Thanks, Amy! I'll give them a call."

"If they don't have any, my mom will know who does," Amy said. "And I'm adding you to my prayer list. For guidance with your career."

It had been a long time since Lexi had had someone praying for her. She crossed the room and hugged Amy. "Thank you. I'm so glad we reconnected."

"I am, too."

They went back downstairs, inspecting all the nooks and crannies on the first floor, before joining Shawn once more. Lexi peppered him with questions about the building's history and if the historical society would be an issue if she wanted to add a kitchen. Finally, they locked the building up, and Lexi and Amy headed to The Beanery to discuss it.

A future back home in Sweet Dreams was looking more promising by the minute.

A knock on his door Tuesday night startled Clint. He'd been mulling over the email he'd opened earlier. The ranch in Montana had finally gotten back to him that yes, they had additional feed and could sell it to him. The price they quoted would have allowed Rock Step Ranch to hold off on selling the calves.

Too late now.

He moved Banjo's head off his lap and yelled, "Who is it?" as he got up.

"Lexi."

Fear and longing slammed into his chest. She rarely came to his cabin. Had she gotten the same email and was here to confront him about it? Or had she thought about his kiss and decided to fire him? He'd only spoken a few words with her since, and those words were merely to let her know the heifer had died.

She stood in the doorway with snow swirling around her, the glow of the porch light surrounding her. He'd never tire of seeing her pretty face.

"Are you busy?"

"No." He stepped backward. "Come in."

She unwound the scarf from her neck and took off her coat. Banjo loped over to her, and she petted him. "Hey, there, buddy. You look pretty content here."

"What's going on?" Clint led her to the living room, turning down the volume on the reality show he'd been watching.

"Amy and I toured the building downtown, and it's even better than I thought. Besides adding a kitchen and updating the bathrooms, I wouldn't have to do any major redesign of the floor space. It does need a lot of TLC and possibly a new heating system, though."

"I don't understand." The building had been a lark, hadn't it? Why would she check it out if her wedding business was in Denver?

"I'm toying with a few options, and buying the building is one of them. When I think of all the women in the area and how they could have special wedding receptions there, it fills me with energy." She took a seat in the chair next to the lit Christmas tree. "I've been having so much fun."

"I'll trust you on that."

She grinned, eyes twinkling. "Oh, come on, one of your girlfriends must have been a romantic. You never did tell me about them."

He'd avoided this topic with her in the past, but maybe it would be best if she knew the truth. Then they could go back to being boss and employee, and his heart would stop jolting every time he saw her face.

"I've never had a serious girlfriend."

"Yeah, right." She rolled her eyes.

"I had a few dates in high school, but when I moved to LFR Ranch, there weren't many women around."

"Okay, but you went into town and attended church, right? There were women there."

"Yeah, but I was focusing on my future. Saving my paychecks. I wasn't thinking about anything serious with a woman."

She sank into the chair, her glow dimming.

"I'm not like other guys. I don't have parents. There will be no doting grandparents for a woman to hope for. No one to throw her a bridal shower. And I'm not exactly the relationship expert."

"Neither am I. I have none of those things to offer a man, either."

"No bridal shower for a groom to be?" He couldn't help trying to make her smile. She had so much more to offer than he did.

"You know what I mean." She reached over and straightened one of the lassos on the tree. "And I always thought Daddy would be around to give me away, but… Well, it doesn't matter. It has nothing to do with the building downtown. It will be for me to plan other people's weddings."

He met her eyes and didn't miss the longing in them.

"You'll plan your own wedding, too. I can tell you're starting to heal from losing your dad. You'll be back to yourself, and…" He couldn't finish his sentence. Couldn't lead her on, but the thought of her eventually marrying someone else made him nauseous.

The way she was looking at him was doing strange stuff to his heart. He wanted to kiss her. Well, lately he wanted to kiss her every time he saw her or thought of her or…

"I need some help, and it's kind of late notice, so if you're busy, I'll ask someone else."

"What is it?" *Please don't let it be anything that gets me within three feet of you.*

"I'm wondering if you would come to the building with me tomorrow. You're so handy, I thought you'd be able to tell me if anything major seems wrong."

A rush of pride spread through his chest. She thought he was handy. Wanted his opinion.

"Sure thing."

"Thanks, Clint. Can you get away for lunch tomorrow and a few hours after?"

"I can." Banjo sat in front of Clint, setting a paw on his knee. He picked the dog up and settled him on the couch. Banjo laid his head on his lap, and Clint stroked his soft fur, massaging his fingers along the dog's spine.

"He's getting worse, isn't he?" Lexi crossed to the couch, petting Banjo's back. His tail thumped a few times.

"He is. I'm trying to keep him comfortable. The vet gave him steroids, but I'm afraid we'll have to say goodbye sooner rather than later."

"He's a good dog. Thank you for taking care of him." She put her coat and boots back on. Wound the scarf around her neck.

"It's been an honor."

And it had been an honor getting to know her, spending these hours alone with her, but the time was drawing short. He could feel it. And he had no idea what the new year would bring, but he knew it couldn't be cozy evenings with Lexi.

While it was for the best, it pained him just the same.

Chapter Ten

"Christmas is in a week and a half." Nash's voice came through Clint's cell phone loud and clear. "Pick a time and get up here. Marshall can't get away any time soon, so it'll just be the three of us."

Clint tucked the phone between his shoulder and ear as he unlocked and opened the side door to the old equipment shed Wednesday morning. He and Logan had finished feeding the cattle, and Clint had noticed footprints in the fresh snow leading to the shed. Without a reason to inspect the building, he'd never entered it before. He doubted anyone had a need to be in here. The keys to the outbuildings hung on a ring in his office, which stayed unlocked during the day, so any of the employees could have accessed this shed.

"You still up at Wade's ranch?" Clint felt along the wall for a light switch, came up with cobwebs and finally found one. The fluorescent bulbs fizzed to life, and dust motes hung in the air. He checked the floor for signs of a recent visitor, but the hard dirt was packed too much to see anything out of the ordinary. Peering to his left then his right, he tried to find anything that shouldn't be there, but nothing stood out.

"Yeah." Nash sounded disgusted. "I'm stuck here another month on doctor's orders. That's why you need to pack a bag for a few days."

"Do you mind waiting until after Christmas? I'll talk with Lexi and try to get away midweek. We should have enough hands to take care of everything."

"All right. Text me when you have a plan."

They caught up for a few more minutes before saying goodbye. Clint surveyed the shed. A trailer, an old tractor, tools that had seen better days and a plow all came into view. Tarps covered bulky items in the back. He squeezed between a rusty vintage tractor and a hay wagon. He still didn't see anything out of the ordinary—not that he knew what he was looking for—but he was curious about what lay under the tarps.

"Clint? Is that you?"

Clint almost jumped, and his heart began racing. "Yeah, Jerry. It's me."

"Thought I saw you come in here. You looking for something?" Jerry stood in the doorway before closing the door and picking his way toward him.

"Footprints through the snow led here. Seemed suspicious."

"Ain't no reason for anyone to be in here. Maybe they stopped in the doorway to get a break from the wind."

"Can't say for sure. Have you been keeping an eye out for Jake?" Since Jerry had returned to work after recovering from pneumonia, Clint had filled him in on the odd circumstances with the cabin and with Jake showing up on his day off. He'd asked Jerry to pay attention to Jake more, to make sure the kid wasn't bringing trouble to the ranch.

"Haven't seen him all week."

"Which is the way it should be. He's scheduled for Saturday and Sunday." Clint hitched his thumb in the direction of the tarps. "What's back there?"

Jerry pulled his jeans up by the belt loops. "I reckon one of them's the sled RJ used to take the girls out on. Let's have a look."

They peeled the tarp back from the first item.

"Well, I haven't seen this gal in a while. Old Betsy was a trouper." Jerry saluted the red-and-white Ford truck. "This F-100 was the purdiest truck I'd seen when RJ bought her, and she did everything we asked of her until it got too much for the old girl. Boy, she brings back memories."

Clint chuckled. "My first car was Shirley. I bonded with the old rust bucket."

"Help me with this here tarp." Jerry moved to the next big tarp, and together they folded it back, revealing a wooden sleigh.

Clint ran his hand along the curves. The sleigh had been painted black with glossy red trim and had a bench large enough to seat two or three people. He circled it, imagining hooking it up to Coco and Charger, the pair of Belgians they relied on to pull the hay sled when the snow got too deep. "When's the last time this was out?"

"Not since RJ's wife passed. He used to hook it up every Christmas Eve and take Lexi and her mama on a sleigh ride. We'd polish it and pile it with blankets. I used to get a kick out of watching them take off. When she was real little, Lexi would take her gloved hand out of her fancy muff and wave at me. So much joy in her darlin' face." Jerry spat on the dirt floor. "Hadn't seen that particular smile in a long time."

Clint could picture her, a little girl with long brown hair and sparkly eyes, sitting under a pile of blankets on this sleigh. If he had a little girl, he'd want to do the same for her. Drive her around the ranch and listen to the swish of the snow.

"Then you came along. Girls are like Christmas trimmings. They're easy on the eyes, and the right one is sweet as a candy cane. I reckon I've seen Lexi light up a few times when we've discussed you."

"You sure your eyes aren't going bad?" Clint teased, but his balance shifted at the thought of Lexi thinking of him as special. "She's lonely. Anybody would make her light up."

"Is that what you're telling yourself?" Jerry propped a cowboy boot on the sleigh runner. "She brought a man back a while ago. I think his name was Doug, but I called him Dud. She didn't light up for him, no sirree."

Good. He didn't like thinking of Lexi with another guy, even one she'd told him about.

"Miss Lexi sure loves planning weddings, but now she's back, well, I'd like to see her stay. I didn't think it was a possibility. With you here…well, maybe she'll change her mind. But you'd better hurry up. Denver won't wait forever."

A weight of cold dread landed in his gut. The mention of Denver should bring relief, but it didn't. Not one bit. And then there was this false impression—first Lexi, now Jerry—they both seemed to think he was someone he wasn't. *And why's that, Romine?*

He should have told them both about his past from the get-go.

"I know what you're hinting at—"

"Who said anything about hinting?"

"You can get that out of your head." Clint dragged the tarp back over the sleigh. "I'm the ranch manager. Nothing more."

"I just think it might be time to get this sleigh out again. Take Miss Lexi for a sleigh ride. Would do her a world of good."

"I'm not the guy you think I am. I've made mistakes."

"Well, who hasn't, boy?"

He leveled a stare at Jerry. "Not like this."

"You murder someone?"

"No."

"Thief? Jail time?"

"No."

"You one of those predators?"

"You know me better than that." Clint glared at him and edged around the sleigh to check for signs anything was amiss. "I lost some property."

Not just any property. *His* property. His dream.

"Is that so?" Jerry was following so close Clint could have given him a piggyback ride. "I know a bit about it myself."

Clint stilled, iced to the core. Had Jerry found out about his deal with the investor?

"Yeah, I guess it was going on forty years ago now, I decided it was time to make something of my life. I was going to take over a small sheep operation near the Montana border. The missus is a smart one. She told me she'd crunched the numbers and didn't see how we could make a profit. Back then my head was harder than a rock. I knew I'd succeed, and I told her so. Bless her heart, she went along with me, and we tried our hand at those sheep."

"It didn't work out?" Nothing seemed odd in the shed, so he gestured for Jerry to follow him to the door.

"That's putting it mildly."

Clint locked the shed back up, and they crossed the gravel driveway, the wind whipping at their coats.

Jerry raised his voice. "We lost money almost immediately, and instead of taking it like a man and figuring out a new plan, I let my pride get the best of me. Took out loans to cover the costs."

"I can relate."

Jerry paused and clapped him on the shoulder. "I lost it all, son."

The emotion pressing against Clint's chest came as a surprise. Felt the hot rush of pain that had stabbed him when he'd found the bank man at his door, telling him he had to move, that they owned the property. Remembered the frantic research he'd done for days, the calls, the need to make sense of it all. The prayers to God not to take away his ranch.

He didn't want Jerry to have lost his dream, too.

"I'm sorry."

"Never felt so ashamed in my life." Jerry braced himself against wind as they strode toward the office. "Thought my wife was going to leave me. I deserved it. She'd told me not to do it, and I hadn't listened."

"But you're still together?"

"Yep. God blessed me with that woman." He continued talking without breaking his stride. "I hadn't told her about the loans. When it all came crashing down and the bank was breathing down my neck, I had to come clean. Worst day of my life."

They reached the door to the ranch office, but Clint didn't open it. "What did she do?"

A lopsided smile lifted the corner of his mouth. "I girded myself for a verbal lashing. And you know what? She gave it to me good. Lit into me for a good hour. I deserved every second of it."

"And then what happened?"

"She slammed out of the house. When she got back later, she told me she'd been praying, and she forgave me."

"Just like that?"

"Just like that."

Clint didn't know much about wives, but Jerry's sounded like one of a kind.

Jerry waggled his glove-encased index finger. "A good woman will forgive you your mistakes. You want to hold onto her when you find her. And take it from me—don't let your yearnings get ahead of your earnings."

It had been almost five years since Clint had allowed himself a yearning. He'd accumulated a lot of earnings in the years since he'd lost it all. Only spent money on rent and his basic needs. The pile of money in the bank was as much as he'd invested into his land originally. But he hadn't thought about spending it. Hadn't dared dream about buying a ranch again. So it sat there and grew.

"Wish I would have known you five years ago. Would have saved me a lot of trouble. I lost it all, too."

Jerry shook his head. "Let it go. It's done. Give it to our good Lord. He forgives everything from a repentant sinner."

"I've repented."

"Then there's nothing holding you back. Now I'm done freezing my toes off out here. You coming in?"

"No, Banjo will be waiting for me."

"It's the ding-dong-iest thing with that dog. Followed RJ around and wouldn't budge. Knew who his master was. Moped along, barely ate in the weeks following RJ's death. And then you show up, and Banjo clings to you like a tick on a deer."

"You're reading into things too much, Jerry." Clint turned to leave.

Jerry chuckled. "And you can't read the signs to save your life, boy."

Clint couldn't argue. It was true.

"Losing the sheep ranch was a real blow. But my pride could have driven away my missus, too. At the end of the day, I didn't lose anything of real value."

Clint frowned, the words not adding up. How could he say he hadn't lost anything of real value? "But the money and your dream..."

"Money comes and goes. Dreams change. I found a job here at Rock Step and met RJ, the best friend I ever had besides my wife. The Lord blessed me right good, and there ain't a day that goes by I don't thank Him for it." Jerry nodded to the door. "There's Banjo."

"I have some errands to run and won't be around until later tonight."

"I hope those errands include Miss Lexi."

"Stop matchmaking and make yourself useful. Tell Logan to keep his eyes open for anything suspicious."

He strode outside with Banjo beside him. Jerry had lost everything years ago, but now he seemed happy and content. He was able to look back and see the blessings from the wreckage. Clint drew his eyebrows together. Were there any blessings from his own mistake?

Did he have to bear the burden of shame about it forever? Or was it time to let it go?

He didn't have time to think about it now. Lexi was waiting for him.

"You're sure you don't mind if I pick out a few gifts?" Lexi glanced over her shoulder at Clint standing behind her in Loraine's Mercantile.

"Nope."

She choked down a laugh at how he was standing, his gaze straight ahead, arms locked down by his sides. He appeared to be trying to mentally transport himself anywhere but here. She, on the other hand, wouldn't mind staying in this cozy shop for hours. With Christmas music playing softly over the loudspeakers and evergreen boughs hung with red ribbons, the store put her in the holiday spirit.

She'd had an ulterior motive for inviting Clint today. Yes, she wanted his advice about the building, but more than that, she needed a few answers before she could think about making a major life change. Unfortunately, the answers couldn't be found by asking direct questions. Not to Clint, anyway.

She needed to spend a little time outside the ranch with him, to see if she was whipping up romantic notions where they didn't exist. Some good conversations, chemistry and mutual interest in the ranch did not equal a lasting love. From what Clint had told her, he wasn't even looking for love.

But what guy was?

If love found him, would he be the kind of man she'd always hoped to find? Or would he be emotionally closed off? Unwilling to share the deepest parts of himself?

"I remember coming in here a few times in high school. Wasn't it a junk store?" Clint picked up a glass paperweight before setting it back down.

"Pinko's Odds N Ends." Lexi checked the price on a tube of lavender lotion. "I don't remember when it changed hands, but Loraine clearly has the style thing going on. I love the rustic chic feel of this place."

"Rustic what?"

"Chic." She pointed to the vintage wooden hutches and tables used for displays. "Elegant with outdoor elements."

"I'll take your word for it."

"Look at these adorable candles." She held the open Mason jar up for him to smell. He didn't move or take a sniff. She raised an eyebrow, shoving it closer to his face, plastering her sweetest smile on her own. It was fun pushing his buttons. "What do you think?"

He inhaled. "Blueberry pie."

"Exactly. I think the girls at work would love this." She added four more candles to her basket, then meandered over to the jewelry. "Oh, wow. This silver is stunning."

She lifted a chain with a bouquet of silver flowers dangling from it. "I've never seen a necklace like this. The flowers are exquisite." She brought it closer, then checked the tag. "Handmade."

Clint sidled up to her. "Yeah, it's nice."

"Nice? It's amazing. I think it's perfect for Amy. We'd better get over to the building. Shawn will be there any minute. Let me pay for these, and we can go."

After making her purchases, they strolled down the sidewalk on their way to the old department store. Neither spoke, and Lexi's mind wandered. One gift she didn't have to worry about? Clint's. She'd called Dan and Lola Smith, and she still couldn't believe she'd been able to put a deposit down on the one puppy they had left. Apparently someone had bought it, then canceled. The best part? It would be available on Christmas Eve.

She sighed in contentment. So far, the day had been lovely. A relaxing lunch with Clint at the sandwich shop. Browsing the mercantile. And now this. She found herself wanting to get closer to him, to tell him some of the things she'd been mulling over lately.

"Do you read the Bible much?" She glanced up at him.

"You come up with the most random topics." He seemed taller right next to her.

"I know, my mind operates in mysterious ways. I've been reading my Bible more."

"And?"

"I'm not as angry about Daddy not telling me."

"That's good."

"Yeah." She shivered against the cold.

"Prayer has kept me going many times over the years."

Could she say the same? "I used to pray regularly. Used to take everything to God."

"You don't anymore?" He extended his arm for her to cross the road.

"I'm starting to, but there were several years when I didn't. I got busy. And excited. I think I was so passionate about my business taking off that I left God out of the picture. Oh, I still prayed at church and before meals, but let's face it, a prayer before dinner isn't really inviting Him into my life, you know."

"I know. I've had periods where I've gotten wrapped up in my own stuff, too."

"Like when?"

"Off and on throughout my life."

"How did you get back into praying?"

He shrugged. "I just did it."

While she was thankful he was willing to have this conversation, he wasn't opening up much to her. She wanted to know more.

"What do you pray for?" she asked.

"Looks like the Realtor arrived." Clint nodded to where Shawn's truck was parked.

So much for digging deeper. She hurried ahead. "Wait until you see the inside."

Clint let the tape measure slide back into its case with a snap. Lexi had been right about this building. It was a gem. A neglected eyesore, but a prize just the same. He'd checked everything he could—the roof needed work and the heating system needed to be replaced altogether, but the electrical system and wiring were fine—and he was jotting notes for Lexi to ask a contractor. Shawn had left an hour ago, telling them to text him when they'd finished.

Lexi waved to Clint from the second-floor balustrade. He grinned up at her. Couldn't help himself. She had dirt smudged on her cheek and the biggest smile he'd ever seen. She was practically skipping around up there, speaking into her phone. She hadn't stopped talking into it since they arrived. At first he'd thought she was calling someone, but she'd told him she was leaving herself voice memos. He didn't even know you could do that on your phone.

Yeah, she was something.

And, as they'd methodically checked the building, he'd enjoyed listening to her prattle on about refinishing the floors, restoring the staircase, converting the first-floor storage room into a kitchen and moving the office to the second floor.

Even better? He'd caught her vision. He could see the building with shining floors and brides and grooms. He could practically hear the laughter of the wedding guests and smell the roasted chicken Lexi claimed was on every bride's menu.

What a gift—to see the world through Lexi's eyes. Her way of seeing things was so different than his, so filled with hope and beauty. She made things the best they could be.

He accepted things as they were. Messy, difficult and unchangeable.

Just being around her made him feel alive.

Eating lunch with her, trailing her through the girlie store, having real conversations with her—they made him want more. He'd caught himself wondering what it would be like to hang out with her on a daily basis. To cook together and watch goofy movies and chat about the ranch and ride horses around the property.

When had she become his idea of perfect?

From the minute she opened the door the day I arrived.

"I'm about done," Lexi called from upstairs. "I'm texting Shawn."

"Yeah, I'm wrapping up, too." He gathered his notes and slipped the tape measure into his pocket.

"All day I've been imagining this staircase." She stood at the top with her hands up. "Okay, go back in time mentally. Picture me in a gown circa 1900. It's a Christmas wedding, so I'm in long sleeves, and the dress is flowing with lace overlays. Sorry, but you're going to have to be the groom in this scenario. So you're in a dark suit. Very dapper. And the lanterns are glowing, it's getting dark and snowflakes are falling outside the windows. The wedding supper is about to begin, and I'm all set to make my grand entrance."

"Wait, is this a wedding today that's imitating 1900, or is it really 1900?" He couldn't believe he was playing along with this. A month ago, he would have refused. But today…it felt right.

"It's 1900. Okay, someone's playing the piano, and the wedding guests are lined at the bottom of the steps." She tipped her chin up, then lifted an imaginary skirt. He had no idea what he was supposed to do, but he sure couldn't wait to see what happened next.

With one hand on the handrail, she glided down, pretending to hold a skirt. Even with the smudge on her cheek, he envisioned her as a bride back in the day. When she had about two steps to go until the bottom, his hands got a mind of their own. He caught her by the waist, swinging her to the floor.

"My, my, you're one strong cowboy." She batted her eyelashes coyly, still in character.

"Wouldn't want the little lady to slip," he said in a deliberately low voice, still holding her waist.

"That's very chivalrous of you." Her eyes gleamed, challenging him. "What now, tiger?"

"Well, it is a Christmas wedding, right?"

Wide-eyed, she nodded.

"Then I reckon there'd be mistletoe hanging above us."

"I reckon there would."

"And the ceremony *is* over."

"Oh, yes. Any self-respecting bride would have had the wedding in the church." She twined her arms around his neck.

"Then, sugar, the only logical conclusion would be this." His voice grew husky, and he pressed his lips to hers. Warm, soft, tasted as sweet as the candy canes hanging from his Christmas tree. She kissed him back, and he held her tightly, wishing time would stand still. Wishing she could be his imaginary mistletoe bride forever.

But nothing lasted forever, and he knew it all too well.

He broke away, still holding her close, not wanting to let go of her, not wanting her to loosen her hold from his shoulders.

She smiled up at him. "If I'd known you were going to kiss me like that, tiger, I would have married you sooner."

He laughed. Only Lexi could come up with the perfect thing to say in this situation. Maybe they could both pretend the kiss had been harmless, a little make-believe on a winter's day.

"If I'd known you tasted as sweet as your name, sugar, I wouldn't have waited so long to kiss you."

The door clanged open, and Lexi jumped back. Clint turned, patting his pockets, pretending he'd lost something. "I think I left my pen in the other room." And he fled to the back.

This had to stop. Playing pretend wedding wasn't smart. His heart was getting too tied up with Lexi. Without him, she'd be fine. But what about him? Life without her… He was beginning to think losing his land had been nothing compared to losing Lexi.

If he never had her, he couldn't lose her. One kiss was as far as it could go.

But he knew he'd forever remember the taste of sugar and the closest thing to a wedding he'd ever have.

Chapter Eleven

"I hate to do this so close to Christmas, but I'm driving to Denver right after our meeting." Lexi waved for Clint to take a seat in her office the next morning. Christmas was a week away, and the questions inside her were eating her alive. Buy the building in Sweet Dreams and stay? Or move back to Denver, back to reality and her company?

She knew what she wanted to do. But what if Clint wasn't interested in pursuing a relationship with her?

"For good?" His blue eyes darkened as he frowned.

"No, I'll be back on Monday." She forced a smile, but inside she was a mess. Staying here if he wasn't interested was unthinkable. He'd been in her office for all of three seconds and already her heart was beating out of control. She'd thought about his kiss a gazillion times. Couldn't stop herself from imagining a future here full-time. Horseback rides. Summer picnics. Snowmobiling in the winter. Showing him the mock-ups for the weddings she'd be planning. Running the ranch. Holding hands. Stealing a kiss or two.

Maybe, just maybe, a wedding of her own.

"Madeline Roth, the senator's daughter I told you about, wants a meeting before hiring me, and I have some things to discuss with my assistant and vice president. The new year will be here before I know it, and I have decisions to make."

"I hope you trust me when I say I will always put the ranch's needs first." He looked so earnest, she wanted to round the desk and caress his cheek. Role playing yesterday had been such an exhilarating surprise. She'd had no idea he would play along so well…and so convincingly. But today he appeared to be as conflicted as she was.

"I don't question it, Clint." She didn't question his loyalty to the ranch, but what about his feelings toward her? She'd never planned her future around a man, and she'd be crazy to create one around someone who might not be interested in the same things she wanted.

"Why aren't you staying in Denver for Christmas?"

"I don't want to." She crossed her arms over her chest. Didn't he want her here? "In fact, I was hoping you'd come to church with me on Christmas Eve. You don't have plans, do you?"

"I'm taking care of the herd so the rest of the crew can celebrate with their families."

"The church service isn't until seven at night. The chores will be done by then."

"Are you sure it won't complicate things even more?"

Comments like that were why she didn't know what to do. His kiss yesterday had taken her to another place—one where she felt safe and cherished and, dare she say, loved. But if he only saw her as a complication, well, she'd be a fool to sell her company and pine for someone who didn't care about her.

"It's church, Clint. A Christmas service."

"I'll pick you up at six thirty."

"So I guess we should discuss the ranch. Anything new I need to know about?"

"Yes, actually." Frowning, he opened the file folder he always brought with him. "I heard back from the ranch in Montana I contacted about buying extra feed this winter. Turns out they could have sold to us. The price was right."

She leaned back, her hands on the armrests. "Well, it doesn't matter now. The calves are sold."

"I should have pushed harder to get an answer." His gaze bored into hers.

"Didn't you call them several times?"

"Yes."

"There's only so much you can do. It's over. No big deal. We have pregnant cows and enough food to get them through winter, and we sold the calves. We're in good shape."

If Clint cared half as much for her as he did the ranch and Banjo, she'd be making an offer on the building downtown today. Why was this decision so difficult?

He'd taken a pen out of his pocket and was jotting something on one of the papers. Watching his long fingers gracefully hold the pen and his forehead furrow in that serious way of his, she caught her breath.

When had she fallen in love with him?

"I know it might not be a possibility this winter, but I'm looking for used farm equipment so we can fill the hay barn next fall. I don't want to be at the mercy of other ranches all the time."

He had no idea her heart was bursting with love even as it deflated from reality.

She'd told herself she wouldn't settle for ho-hum.

And being around Clint was never dull. The breathless kisses he had down, but what about the other things she wanted—someone who loved her enough to make a grand gesture and who wanted marriage and kids?

If breathless kisses were all she'd get from Clint, maybe she should move back to Denver.

He'd be spending Christmas Eve with Lexi. And he had no idea what to get her for Christmas. Did he buy her a gift an employee would give—something impersonal like a canister of cashews? Or did he follow his heart and buy her chocolates, roses, jewelry—things that shouted *Lexi*?

Neither, you fool.

Clint finished mucking Nugget's stall and moved on to the one next to it. He was on cleanup duty, which suited him fine. Good, hard work might take his mind off the brown-haired, brown-eyed girl who burrowed into his thoughts night and day.

When he'd said goodbye after their meeting, he'd wanted to yank her close to him and kiss her again.

Those kinds of wants were coming at him more and more.

Was this what love felt like? *Love.* He snorted. This wasn't love. It was infatuation. A guy like him would fall for any girl who looked at him twice. It was proximity, loneliness…

It felt like love.

The clink of the pitchfork hitting glass stopped him. *What in the world?*

He dug through the hay and found an empty pint bottle of whiskey. He ground his teeth together as he held up the offending bottle. Same as the ones he'd found in the old cabin.

Whoever had been in the cabin had surely been here, too.

He texted Logan to come to the barn.

His gut told him Jake was to blame, but he didn't have evidence, and in the past, he'd been accused of crimes he didn't commit.

Logan entered the stables.

"Look what I found." Clint held the bottle up.

Logan looked taken aback, then his lips firmed into a thin line.

"Any ideas who it might belong to?" Clint asked.

"I've got an idea, but I don't have proof."

"Name?"

"Jake. Ryder's been reliable." Logan frowned. "He has been hanging out with Jake more, though. I don't think it's him, but to be fair… Well, you know how it is."

"Is Ryder here?"

"Checked in at 6:00 a.m. He wanted extra money for Christmas—I think he's got a girlfriend—so I told him to come in an hour before school this week and next. Hope that's okay. I probably should have mentioned it to you yesterday."

"It's fine. I would have done the same."

They stared at the bottle a minute, the nickering of horses the only sound.

"I'm not sure how to handle this, Logan. I can't tolerate drinking, but without any proof of who did this, my hands are tied."

Logan scratched the stubble on his chin. "I was thinking the same. Whoever left this is clearly drinking here. And stupid enough to leave the bottle around."

"I have caught Jake here when it wasn't his shift. And he claimed he was mucking stalls. I didn't buy it, but a phone call made me forget to come back and check the area."

"Well, I guess we'll have to have a talk with him tomorrow morning. That's his next shift, right?"

"Yep." Clint leaned against the stall frame. "Send him to my office when he arrives. I'll show him the bottle and ask if it's his."

"Want me to get Ryder in here? Ask him a few questions?"

"No. Let's wait to see what happens with Jake first."

Clint took the bottle back to his office and slipped it inside his file cabinet drawer next to the petty cash. Then he locked the cabinet and headed back out to the stables to finish cleaning. Letting the matter go didn't sit well with him. He wanted to find out who dared drink in the stables. Boot him off the property. Drunks could be a danger to everyone on the ranch, including the animals, but most of all, inebriated men posed a threat to Lexi.

For the first time since she'd left yesterday, he was glad she was in Denver. Safe from harm. He'd do whatever it took to keep her safe. He wished he could keep her safe forever.

"I'm concerned if I hire you, you won't be available for my needs. I'm wary of a wedding planner not being in the same state." Madeline Roth's posture would put a debutante to shame. Wearing a pale gray pantsuit and lavender silk blouse, matching lavender heels and with her blond hair smoothed into an elegant chignon, she projected confidence and sophistication.

Had the previous two hours of pitching wedding

themes been for nothing? Lexi forced her smile to stay in place. She wasn't even sure she wanted to plan Madeline's wedding. "That's a valid concern, but let me assure you I do what it takes to keep my clients happy. I have an office in Wyoming, and I'm in constant contact with my staff."

"Oh." The word was loaded with negative implications. "Does this mean you're not planning on returning to Denver?"

Tough question. "I will know after the holidays."

"I'm interested in working with you *if* you decide to move back. I'm not comfortable hiring you if you'll be splitting time between here and Wyoming. Carson and I will be out of the country until January 2. We won't be making a decision until then. I'll call you when we're back." Madeline stood, and Lexi walked her to the door.

"I appreciate your honesty. I hope we'll be working together soon."

As soon as Madeline left, Lexi dropped into her chair, propped her elbows on the desk and let her forehead fall into her hands. Madeline had been her final appointment of the day. Lexi had put a lot of thought and effort into the themes she'd pitched to Madeline, but now that they'd met, she couldn't muster the same excitement as before.

Devoting so much energy to demanding brides never used to bother her.

But now?

The sixty-hour workweeks before Daddy died came to mind. She was tired. She'd had no life of her own in years.

Her thoughts switched to riding horses with Clint and sipping coffee with Amy. To her pretty office at the ranch and the ideas she'd been toying with to remodel the ranch house and the old department store in Sweet Dreams. Shawn Lesly had called her earlier and told her he'd talked to the listing agent. The owner loved the idea of a reception hall and was willing to negotiate on the price.

She'd hoped coming back to Denver for the weekend would remind her what she'd be giving up, but so far, it had only made her want to return to Wyoming as soon as possible.

Her gaze fell to the phone on her desk. She'd been sitting right here in July when Daddy had called. *I'm thinking about going to Yellowstone next month. Want to join me? It's been years since we hiked Mystic Falls Trail.*

He'd taken her to Yellowstone many times, and Mystic Falls was their favorite spot. She cringed, remembering her reply. *I'd love to, Daddy, but I'll have to wait until next summer. I'm booked for months.*

Booked for months.

Some daughter.

Her throat felt tight, scratchy, and today had been bad enough without adding tears. She took a drink of water from the bottle on her desk.

Nothing was going according to plan.

Oh, who was she kidding? She didn't have a plan. She'd been living on a whim ever since the funeral. And it was time to get back on track.

Today had been rough from the start. Jolene had called off with the flu, so Lexi had been stuck with hours of administrative duties. And while she'd heaved a sigh of relief that the offices were neat this time, the storage room was a mess. Each planner had shelves for their orders, but boxes had been stacked on the floor, making it difficult to move around. And some of the shelves were empty. How hard was it to put a box on a shelf? Not much more difficult than setting it on the floor.

She'd only seen one planner in the office all day, which wasn't unusual if the others had weddings scheduled for the weekend, but Natalie didn't have one on the books. Why wasn't she here?

And every time Lexi had walked past the front desk, her blood boiled. The flowers were still wrong. They were *not* blush-colored blooms. They were red roses. Red! Again. She'd trusted Natalie to handle the problem, but it hadn't been dealt with.

It had taken every ounce of her self-control not to throw them in the trash and order the blush-colored bouquets.

"Lexi, you're back." Natalie Allen, a tall redhead in a black pencil skirt and fitted emerald blouse, entered the room. She took a seat opposite Lexi and placed her cell phone and planner on the desk.

Lexi took a deep breath to calm her agitation. She checked the time. It was after six.

While the cat's away, the mice will play.

"Why are there red roses on the front desk?" Lexi flattened her palms on the desk. "You assured me you would take care of fixing the order. This is the second time I've been here this month, and both times I've seen red roses. What is going on?"

Natalie lifted her chin as her cheeks flushed. "The other designers and I thought red brought a more festive air to the office. It *is* Christmas."

Lexi's fingers curled into her palms. Was she imagining the challenge in Natalie's tone? And since when did all the designers change the rules? None of them had invested their money in this company, worked sixty- to eighty-hour weeks to build the best reputation possible. She straightened. "Every Christmas the florist adds silver branches and mint-colored greens for a more subdued holiday look. The color scheme is important for our brand."

"Maybe it's time for a change."

Lexi blinked. She counted to three, trying to control her temper. "If a change were to be made, it would be *my* decision. These details matter to me. They're important. And looking around, I see other things being neglected. You told me you would handle them."

"I'll make a note." Not appearing overly concerned, Natalie checked her phone. "How did the meeting with Ms. Roth go? If you think you'll be in Wyoming and unable to accommodate her needs, I'm available. Her wedding is *the* wedding to land. I have so many ideas."

Lexi gaped at her. Didn't Natalie care what the other details being neglected were? And had she really just tried to undercut the Roth wedding from her?

"I don't know where to go with that comment at this moment." Lexi didn't even try to keep the incredulity out of her tone. She sat back in her chair, setting her elbow on the armrest and letting her cheek rest against her index finger. "Am I missing something? When I left in October, this place was running smoothly, and now I'm getting complaints from our clients. I see problems."

Natalie scoffed. "Brides always complain if the day doesn't go exactly the way they'd hoped. They're impossible to please."

"Maybe so, but these complaints have been valid. Missing invitations, the wrong place settings, no photographer showing up?"

"I haven't had any complaints from my clients."

"But you're the VP. Every client is my responsibility and yours."

"I think we're all adults here, and each planner should be responsible for her own clients. If you hired a purchaser..."

"My name is on every contract. This is my reputation."

Natalie pursed her lips.

Lord, I'm not getting through to her. What happened? We used to be on the same page, but now she acts like I'm insane for having standards. I don't know if I want to do this anymore. Let the flowers be red, and the boxes be shoved anywhere the planners want. Let them figure out their own insurance and come up with their own expense accounts. I'm so tired of managing them. I want a life. What do I do? Show me the way.

Something changed—a wave of peace settled over her like a warm ray of sunshine. She turned her head and studied her office, the hall beyond it and Natalie looking like she'd been sucking on a lemon.

"Natalie, where do you see yourself in five years?"

Natalie jerked to attention. "Sounds like a job interview question."

"Maybe it is."

She tipped her chin up. "I see myself as one of the top designers in Denver. I've landed several influential couples in the past three years, and I've been positioning myself to be the go-to designer for the crème de la crème. Not only here, but throughout the state." She held herself proudly.

Lexi bit her lower lip. Natalie's goals weren't terrible, but they didn't fit with the Weddings by Alexandra philosophy. Lexi had always prided herself on planning weddings for every budget. She enjoyed making the dreams of all her brides come true, not just the ones with the most money or status.

The truth stared her in the face. Her business would not thrive unless she moved back and made changes to her staff.

Lexi studied the office she'd put so much thought into decorating, and for the first time, it felt impersonal. Worse, it stifled her. These four walls contained so much responsibility.

"Have you thought about going off on your own?" Lexi asked.

A flicker of unease lit her eyes. "It's crossed my mind on occasion. Why?"

"I'm thinking about making a change. Like you suggested."

"Look, Lexi," Natalie said quickly, "I'm sorry about the flowers. I should have checked with you before changing the order."

"Don't worry. I'm not firing you." She tidied the papers on her desk. "I'm seriously considering moving to Wyoming for good. If I did, I would keep the Weddings by Alexandra brand, but I would sell this building. You and I have worked together for a long time, and frankly, I don't think we see eye to eye when it comes to the company anymore. If I sell, I'm giving you the first right to make an offer on it. I don't know if you'd want to set up a company the way I did or rent space to other planners. You'd have to figure it out for yourself. If I don't sell, we're going to have to schedule a meeting to get on the same page."

Natalie paled. "You'd sell this to me?"

"Yes."

"I... I never thought..." She blinked a few times. "I'm honored you're giving me the first right."

"Do you have the capital to consider this? I can recommend a financial adviser to help you come up with a business plan."

"I can raise the money. Are you serious? I mean, really serious about possibly selling? I don't want to get my hopes up for nothing."

"I'm not giving you false hope. Get a business plan together. Even if I ultimately don't sell, your work won't be for nothing. Maybe this is what you need. I have a feeling you want more control, and that's why so many details are being ignored around here. Maybe you resent the fact that I make the rules. Or maybe I'm way off base. I don't know. I do know things change, and we have to change with them." Lexi stood, yawning. "Now, if you'll excuse me, I have a date with a burrito platter."

After locking up and picking up takeout from her favorite Mexican restaurant, she admired the city's glittering Christmas lights on her way home to her condo. She'd long loved Denver, but her life here had become all work all the time. She climbed the steps to the front door, turned on the lights, changed into sweats and switched the television on to enjoy her burrito with a Christmas movie.

Thirty minutes later the half-eaten food had been pushed aside, and she turned off the television. There wasn't anything good on, and a restlessness had been building inside her ever since she talked with Natalie.

How could she have gone from living her dream to ready to sell her company in a few short months? What happened?

Clint Romine. He's what had happened.

And worse, she was ready to move back home and live on the ranch when it was too late to spend time with her father. Why couldn't she have gotten this urge last year, when it would have mattered and she could have enjoyed being with her dad?

If he were here now, what would she say to him? *Well, Daddy, it's like this. There's a super-cute cowboy, and he took over the ranch for me. He's reliable, and I trust him, and I like being with him, although I'm pretty sure I drive him nuts sometimes. He's quiet. Gets things done. And he kissed me. It was a good kiss. I can't stop thinking about it.*

And what could her father possibly say in response? *What about the business you sacrificed so much time and money for? I'd hate to see you throw it all away for a guy, especially a cowboy. Didn't I warn you about them? He'll only break your heart, Lexi.*

Oh, what do you know, Daddy? I'm in love!

She yanked a throw off the edge of the couch and spread it over her lap. *Fantastic.* She was having imaginary conversations with her deceased father where she sounded like a silly teenager. And she was arguing with him, no less. Inhaling a long breath, she counted to four then exhaled.

Her brain was useless. What she needed was divine guidance.

Lord, thank You for opening my eyes to the reality of Weddings by Alexandra. I want to be sad my heart isn't here in Denver anymore and the company You blessed me with doesn't jolt me out of bed with excitement the way it used to. I know changes are coming—and they're needed. But I don't know if I should start fresh in Wyoming with a new wedding planning business and a pos-

sible future with Clint, or if I should move back here and make hard choices about my current staff.

Lexi opened the Bible app on her phone and scrolled through the topics before stopping on one. She read Philippians chapter two, about being united in Christ. Instead of continuing on, she circled back to verses three and four of the second chapter. *Do nothing out of selfish ambition or vain conceit. Rather, in humility value others above yourselves, not looking to your own interests but each of you to the interests of the others.*

The verses were about how to treat fellow Christians, but they could have been written to describe her father. He always treated his employees as family, anticipating their needs and looking out for them. He'd worked hard his entire life to build the ranch into a large, profitable operation, but not out of selfish ambition. He'd told her time and again to offer first fruits to the Lord, that all they had was from Him alone. He'd drilled it into her that using her talents to the best of her ability was a way to honor God.

She burrowed under the throw. Selfish ambition described her. She could have made the time to spend a weekend hiking in Yellowstone with her dad. No wonder he hadn't told her about the cancer. She'd put her job above him for years.

Lord, forgive me for my selfishness. Help me change. Help me be the person You want me to be.

A few months ago, she'd believed she was exactly where she was supposed to be. And now? So many options. Sell the business. Open a new one. Stay here. And do what with the ranch?

Too much to think about right now. What would be

best for Clint? For Natalie? For her other employees, like Jolene? Logan? *Ugh.*

Her lawyer had agreed to a meeting tomorrow morning, even though it was Saturday. Maybe she'd get some answers then. Risking it all had never been her strong suit.

Chapter Twelve

As dusk fell Monday evening, Clint finished his rounds and headed back to the office to lock up. Jake hadn't shown up for work on Saturday or Sunday, and he and Logan figured they'd seen the last of him. And after watching Lexi's car drive up to the main house an hour ago, Clint hoped Jake was the one who'd left the bottle. He didn't like having an unknown threat around the ranch, and he really hadn't liked the way his heart had somersaulted when he'd seen Lexi's car.

Just get through Christmas Eve with her. She's probably moving back to Denver, anyway. Then you can concentrate on the ranch without all these distractions.

Like her pretty eyes, her laugh, her kindness. Her soft hair, the feel of her slim waist in his hands, the way her lips tasted as sweet as syrup. Man, he missed her.

He took his gloves off and slapped them against his thigh, yanked open the office door and stopped in his tracks.

"What do you think you're doing?"

Jake stood over the file cabinet with the petty cash box in his hands and guilt etched into his face. Even if the kid didn't reek of hard liquor, the way he swayed and his bloodshot eyes left no uncertainty he was drunk.

"Just filing some papers, boss." He tried to discreetly drop the petty cash back into the cabinet, but it fell with a thud.

"You're fired."

"What?" He slammed the drawer shut. "Why?"

Fury shot through Clint's veins, but he'd been practicing keeping his temper in check since he was four years old.

"You're drunk. And you're stealing."

"I don't know what you're talking about."

"Call someone to pick you up, or I'll find you a ride in a squad car."

Jake stumbled toward him, getting in his face. "What's your problem, man? I'm not botherin' you."

Clint stood his ground, staring Jake right in the eye. "I know you used illegal drugs and were drinking during work hours. You're only, what, eighteen? You've got your whole life ahead of you. Don't throw it away on this garbage."

"It's not work hours now."

"Then you have no reason to be here."

Jake glared, swaying, then pulled his fist back, but Clint caught it, twisting the kid's arm under him. "That's it. I'm calling the cops."

"No! I'll leave. I'll drive away right now."

"You're not driving, dummy. I can't have you kill anyone out there. You've put enough people in danger." He let go of his arm. "Here, call your friend." He held out his phone, but Jake chopped down on his arm, sending the phone crashing to the floor, and took off.

"Hey, get back here!" Clint ran after him, but the kid

was fast. He chased him past the barns to the parking lot, but Jake didn't turn. He ran toward the main house.

Lexi!

Clint dug deep and channeled every ounce of energy he had, surging forward and tackling Jake. He hauled him to his feet and dragged him by the arm back toward the office. Jake kicked at him and tried to escape, but Clint kept an iron grip on his arm and didn't slow down.

Logan ran toward them as they passed the stables. "What's going on?"

"Call the police. Then join us in the office."

Logan looked taken aback, but he nodded.

Clint shoved Jake into the office chair and blocked his path. His thoughts couldn't keep up with the pounding of his heart.

"Aw, let me go, man. I'll leave. Never come back. Don't get the cops involved. Please!"

He wouldn't feel sorry for him—didn't feel sorry for him. This was for the safety of Rock Step Ranch. And Jake had it coming.

"Hey, I tried to let you go easy. You haven't shown up for work. You come here and use the Harringtons' property as if it was your own personal seedy playground. Why are you messing around with this junk?"

Jake sniffled. "My grandma died a few months ago—"

"And you're honoring her memory by drinking, drugging and stealing? You'll have to come up with something better than that."

He wiped his nose with the back of his hand. "You're heartless."

"I know I am."

"You never liked me. You don't know what I'm going through."

Clint crossed his arms over his chest, his legs wide. "Save the sob story for someone else. I'm your boss. And if I don't make sure you're punished, I'm afraid you won't learn your lesson. You'll hire in at the next ranch and abuse their trust. Keep on with your drinking. Steal to support your habit. And maybe no one will be around to stop you next time, and you'll really hurt someone. You want that on your conscience? I don't want it on yours or mine. When you break the rules, there are consequences. And you broke them. Big-time."

"I won't do it again, I promise."

"Why don't I believe you?"

"I want to talk to Lexi." The slurring returned. "Let her hear my side of the story."

At hearing her name on Jake's lips, Clint balled his hands into fists but kept them down by his sides. "No," he said through clenched teeth.

"Says who? You ain't my boss anymore. Just said so yourself."

Clint flexed his hands and tried to control the anger pulsing through his veins. "If you ever get within a hundred yards of her, I'll rope you like a spring calf and drag you up and down this property for fun. Got it?"

Jake's face turned a greenish hue.

Clint bent to look him in the eye. "Do. You. Understand?"

His Adam's apple worked as he nodded. "Yes."

"Yes, what?"

"Yes, sir."

"Good."

They sat in silence for several minutes until Logan and two officers entered the office. Clint answered their questions, and ten minutes later, one of the officers led a handcuffed Jake away.

"You pressing charges?" the other officer asked. "He doesn't have any priors, but he sure had plenty of excuses for tonight. Makes me wonder how many times he's sweet-talked his way out of trouble."

"I'll have to talk to my boss first." Clint followed him back to the squad car. "It's her call."

"Well, let's hope this experience scares him into getting his act together." They shook hands, and moments later, the police car was on its way off the ranch.

As much as he dreaded this, Clint had to tell Lexi what was going on, and it couldn't wait. He felt like such a fool. His gut had been telling him Jake was a problem, but he'd ignored it and look what had happened. Lexi could have been hurt. Robbed. Worse.

He put his hands on top of his head and looked up at the stars starting to light the sky. His inaction was unacceptable. Last time, his bad judgment had only hurt him. This time, it could have hurt Lexi.

God, forgive me.

She was doing this! Really doing it! Lexi finished unpacking her suitcase, took her earbuds out and headed back downstairs for a cup of tea and a muffin. She'd stopped in at her favorite bakery in Denver before driving back today. The weekend had given her so much clarity. The meeting with the lawyer had revealed more than what would be involved with selling her business; it had shown her what she truly wanted.

Clint made her feel important, special. He anticipated her needs, cared about her safety and looked at her like she was the most beautiful woman in the world. Sure, he hadn't swept her off her feet or even told her how he felt about her, but that was understandable given his upbringing. If she told him she loved him, he'd then feel safe enough to share his feelings.

She opened the bakery box. Triple chocolate chunk, poppy seed or white-chocolate raspberry? Triple chocolate always won. A knock on the door startled her. Taking a bite of muffin, she hurried to the door.

Clint stood before her, throbbing with pent-up energy and looking disheveled. "Sorry to bother you right now."

"What happened?" She dragged him inside. "You look upset."

He took his hat off and stood there with his jaw clenching in and out.

"Come back to the living room where it's warm." Her nerves began ratcheting. What was going on? She didn't even know where to start guessing. "Sit."

He obliged by lowering his body into the chair, and she sat on the couch. "It's Jake. I…" He raked his fingers through his hair. "I had to fire him. The police were involved."

"Oh, my!" She set the muffin down. "Tell me everything."

Clint explained about finding the empty liquor bottle in the stall and his suspicions about Jake. Then he told her about their encounter tonight. "Initially, I planned on firing him and letting him go, but when he ran to your house, I had Logan call the cops. Your safety is too important. I told the officers it was up to you if you wanted to press charges."

Lexi crossed to where he sat, and she slid her arms around his shoulders, hugging him. "I'm so sorry you had to deal with all this."

He edged out of her embrace and rose. He walked to the Christmas tree and touched one of the ornaments.

"I should have fired him when I first suspected he was the one drinking."

"Without evidence? That's not our way, and it's not yours, either."

"Don't you see?" He spun and rushed back to her side in two strides, clasping her upper arms. "He could have hurt you. I know what drinking does to people. Some only need the thinnest excuse to take whatever they want."

"But he didn't hurt me." She wanted to soothe him. He was so close physically, but so far away emotionally. "You took care of it. You did the right thing."

She reached on her tiptoes and pressed her lips to his cheek. How she wanted to take away the misplaced guilt he carried.

"If I'd followed through with my suspicions earlier, we could have avoided this. Now he might be facing jail time."

"Hey." She placed her hand on his chest. "You did nothing wrong. I'll go into the station tomorrow and talk to the officers. From what you've told me, I think spending the night in jail will do Jake a world of good. I don't have to press charges, and I probably won't."

"I think I scared him."

"I'm sure you did. Now wait here. I'm getting you a muffin and telling you my news." She padded back to the kitchen, then returned with the white-chocolate raspberry pastry. She handed it to him, but he set it on the coffee table.

"Lexi, I don't know. Maybe you should consider pressing charges. What if he's vindictive? He knows his way around here. He's snuck in without us knowing on more than one occasion. I caught him trying to steal the petty cash. And when he's drunk, he's mean."

"Okay." She lifted her hands, palms out, to her chest. "The police have him, so we don't need to worry about it anymore tonight."

The vein in his forehead bulged, but he picked up the muffin. A good sign.

"I have some news." She stayed on her feet, pacing away from him to collect her thoughts. Then she pivoted, feeling happy and light. "I'm selling my business in Denver, putting an offer in on the building downtown and moving back for good!"

The muffin dropped out of Clint's hand and rolled under the coffee table. She was moving back.

Selling her business.

And starting over.

Here.

His chest filled with concrete, and it was hardening by the second.

"I realized I've met my goals in Denver. I built a good reputation, and I planned a lot of beautiful weddings, but I'd let my professional goals completely crowd out my life." She moved over to him, took his hands in hers—her eyes gleaming with excitement—and beckoned him to his feet. He rose out of his chair. "I want a life, Clint. A life here. I realize how much I've been missing. Simple things, like riding around the ranch on horseback and spending time with friends. You. Amy. Feeling like I'm part of a community. You know?"

He looked into her trusting, hopeful brown eyes and knew what he had to say was going to fill those eyes with disgust. Tears. Hatred, even.

"But that's not all," she said. "I could do without the horseback rides and being part of a community, but I've come to care for you. Well, more than care, really. I trust you, and not in a you're-a-great-manager way. I've been falling—"

"Lexi."

"What?" She tilted her head, still staring at him like he was someone worth confiding in. Staring at him as if she loved him.

"Sit down."

"Why?"

"Just sit."

"You're scaring me." She sat on the couch.

"You have the wrong impression of me, and it's my fault you have it. The way you're looking at me is the way every guy dreams a girl will look at him, but I don't deserve it."

"What are you getting at?"

"Let me finish." He swallowed, still standing, trying to figure out how to start. "You remember how I told you I lost my land?"

She nodded.

"I didn't tell you all of it. I left out the most important part."

She clasped her hands, wringing her fingers, consternation dipping her eyebrows.

"All those years at LFR, I saved every penny I made. My dream was to own my own cattle ranch. I didn't care how small. I wanted land that was mine, land no one could take away from me. Five years ago, a property came on the market. It had three run-down outbuildings, a fenced-in pasture and a house so beat-up it could have been demolished and it would have looked better. The house didn't matter to me. But the property came with cattle."

He could still feel the rush of excitement when he'd found out about the ranch. If he could go back in time and tell his younger self to think it through…

Shaking his head, he continued. "The owner had died, and the son wanted no part of ranching. I didn't have enough money for the down payment. The bank needed twice as much as I had. So, defeated, I went to the local bar and grill, thinking there was no way I'd be able to buy it."

Why hadn't he trusted God with the timing? Why had he been in such a rush? He could have worked five more years and raised the money. But he hadn't. His chin dropped to his chest. He dreaded telling her the rest.

"I met a man named Devon Fields. By the end of the night, he was my business partner. We worked it out that he'd buy the property. Then he'd sell it to me on a land contract. He said my down payment was enough for him, and I would be paying him back plus interest in monthly installments instead of the bank. I figured it was more than fair. In the light of morning, I had my doubts, but I ignored them. And everything went smoothly, the way Devon said it would."

Lexi leaned forward, chewing on her fingernail. He girded his shoulders, ready for her reaction to what he had to say next.

"Imagine my surprise six months later when the property was foreclosed on. Devon had purchased the property with a mortgage, and instead of using my money and his own for the down payment, he'd obtained an illegal silent second mortgage. The land contract had been built on a lie. He took all my cash and ran. Made two mortgage payments. Two. Then he just disappeared, leaving me with nothing and the bank with the property."

His chest burned at the memory of that time. The disbelief, the helplessness. He'd hired a lawyer and found out Devon Fields wasn't even the guy's real name. There had been nothing he could do to get his land or money back.

"Oh, Clint. I'm so sorry. That's horrible." She stood, her eyes stricken.

"It was my own fault. Who in the world would ever agree to something as stupid as that? My greed blinded me. I should have told you the day you hired me. I've been so ashamed over losing the land. I thought I would be fine managing your ranch, letting you make the big decisions, but I'm not. I got a lousy price for your calves. I lost the heifer when I should have been here, and now I've let a drunken thief do whatever he wants on your property."

He threw his hands to his forehead and ran them over his hair. He had to let her go, and to do that, he had to leave. "I can't do this anymore. Consider this my two weeks' notice."

"You're quitting?" Lexi could barely take it in. "I don't understand."

"I'm done. Two weeks should give you enough time to find a new manager. I'll pack up and be ready to leave the way I should have left right when you hired me."

All the compassion she'd been holding in dissolved at his clipped words.

"Why? Some jerk cons you out of your dream, and you're suddenly not capable of ranching? That's the stupidest thing I've ever heard."

"Well, guess what? You're right on the mark. I'm the stupidest guy you've ever met."

"I didn't call you stupid." But she sure was thinking it right now. What would make him think he had to quit?

"You might as well have. I certainly call myself that and more on a daily basis."

"You shouldn't. You're not stupid. You were tricked. And you've been the best manager I could have ever hoped for here."

"No, I haven't." He looked at the ceiling. "I couldn't get the extra feed we wanted, couldn't get you better prices, couldn't stop Jake from drinking here constantly, and I couldn't even admit to you who I really am. I'm not the man for this job."

"No one could have gotten better prices or extra feed or stopped a cow from dying."

"Look, you've built me into a guy I'm not. If I don't quit, I'll let you down."

"What do you think you're doing now?"

"Not like this… It will be worse. I can't explain it—it's just how it is."

"You can't explain it?" Her voice rose. "It's how it is, huh? I deserve an explanation. We connected. You felt it, too. I know you feel it."

"You're lonely." He didn't meet her eyes.

"So are you."

"I've been lonely my entire life. I can live with it."

She wasn't getting through to him. It was as if a rock wall had formed behind his eyes. What was he so afraid of?

Me. He's afraid of a relationship with me.

She had to talk some sense into him.

"I don't want you to leave. I don't want you to be lonely, Clint. You're scared. I am, too. What I just told you about moving back and starting fresh? Having me here all the time probably terrifies you. But I've been honest with you from day one, Clint Romine. I want this… Wyoming…and you."

"And I've lied to you from day one."

"You haven't lied to me." She wanted to growl in frustration. "You're lying to yourself."

"About what?" He let out a fake laugh.

"About me. About what's between us."

"There can't be anything between us. I'm your manager—your former manager—just a worthless brat, an orphan, a nobody who never belonged to anyone. You think I could really belong here with you? You're ranch royalty. I'm nothing."

"I can't even respond to that. Does how I feel matter at all to you? I'm an orphan, too. And I'm no royalty. I'm a woman who was so busy chasing her professional dreams, I forgot what was important to me."

"You need someone better."

"The fact you just said that makes me wonder if I made a big mistake."

"Oh, honey, you made a mistake."

"Don't call me honey." If she told him she loved him, he'd toss it back in her face. She couldn't get through to him, and she was done trying. "Why don't you go? Go cut yourself off from everyone. It's easier, isn't it? Then you don't have to take a chance and get your heart broken again."

"I told you I don't have a heart."

"You're right. Because all these weeks when I've been opening up to you and telling you personal things, the secrets I didn't want anyone knowing? I was trusting you. And you didn't trust me back."

"I trust you."

"No, you don't." She gaped at him. "If you trusted me, you would have opened up to me. You would have told me the scary things inside you, the ones you don't want anyone to know. You kept the truest part of yourself from me. And now that you finally tell me your secrets, you're leaving. Running away. Unacceptable."

"I know. That's what I've been trying to tell you."

"I understand protecting yourself. I do. But I'm being real tonight, whether you're willing to join me or not. I know why Daddy didn't tell me he had cancer. He figured I'd blow him off for my job. I only have myself to blame." She spun away from him, hating the tears pressing against her eyes. "When you're sitting by yourself each night, you're going to realize you only have yourself to blame, too."

His hands touched her shoulders, but she flinched.

"Your dad knew you loved him," Clint said gently. "He probably didn't want to burden you. He might have thought he had all the time in the world. That was all. He wasn't punishing you."

"Just leave," she whispered.

The sound of his footsteps grew faint. The click of the front door shutting unleashed her tears. She dropped to her knees and covered her face with her hands.

When would she learn? Every time she got something she really wanted, something she loved was ripped away from her.

Her punishment for wanting it all.

Chapter Thirteen

Clint slammed the front door to his cabin as hard as he could and tossed a bag with a change of clothes into his truck. His lungs burned, were closing in on him, but he peeled out of the drive and sped away from the ranch without a second glance. She wanted him to leave? No problem. He'd leave.

He couldn't spend another second on Rock Step Ranch.

The past half hour flogged him. He'd known she'd been on the brink of telling him she loved him, and he'd snapped. Had laid his own sorry past out for her to see. Had done the honorable thing by putting in his notice. Tomorrow she'd wake up and realize what a mistake it had been to develop feelings for someone who had been so dumb. She'd probably be embarrassed she'd gotten involved with him. He'd avoid her as much as possible the next two weeks.

He thumped his fist on the steering wheel. Thirty years of anger and self-loathing churned inside him. Why couldn't he have been raised in a stable home? Had a parent or two who actually cared about his needs? In all the foster homes he'd lived in, he'd never—not once—been so much as considered for adoption.

And no matter how hard he tried, he couldn't convince himself he was anything more than the kid who'd been yelled at and neglected by his grandfather, torn from Miss Joanne and her warm home, shifted from one overworked foster family to another until landing at Yearling.

Rock Step Ranch felt like home, but he'd known from day one it wasn't his. Could never be his.

What is wrong with me? Why am I fundamentally different from everyone else?

He let out a cynical laugh. He'd fallen in love with Lexi, and he didn't even know what love looked like. It was more than discussing the ranch and decorating Christmas trees. It was more than a kiss under the mistletoe.

It was bringing a woman flowers and taking her out for dinner. Listening to her talk about her day, driving her to church, helping her with whatever she needed.

He stared through the windshield at the stars dotting the sky as the truck created distance from the ranch. Love was more than all that, too. Lexi had it right back there. She wanted his secrets. She wanted the deepest part of him, but she wouldn't be able to handle it. He'd bricked the vital parts up and mortared them shut long ago.

Maybe he couldn't handle the deepest parts of himself, either.

The miles sped by as memory after memory of his childhood came back. Running from his grandfather, not being fast enough to avoid the slap of his leather belt across his back and legs. Making cookies with Miss Joanne, sitting on her lap, waiting for her to kiss his hair. Hiding in his bedroom to avoid taking a beating from the kid at the final foster home and taking the beating anyhow. Mucking stalls at Yearling, thankful for a bed and food.

More memories came back. More recent ones. Checking into a dive motel the day he'd been kicked off his property. Curling up on the lumpy bed and crying for hours. A grown man, crying. He should be ashamed of that memory, but he wasn't. Maybe he'd been crying for more than the land. Maybe he'd cried for his entire youth.

Man, he had to stop thinking. Had to cut his losses and move forward. He'd done it so many times, he should be the expert. He switched the radio on, but Christmas songs depressed him. He turned it back off.

The lonely country road enveloped his truck. If only his mind would stay as empty as the blacktop ahead. He couldn't face thoughts of Lexi. Not yet.

A sign appeared stating the next town. He was a few miles from the property he'd lost. How had he ended up here? Funny, he'd thought he'd never want to see it again, but more than anything right now, he did.

After turning down the gravel road where the ranch stood, he drove slowly until he reached the land that had once been his. He drove beyond the pasture and passed the house. Even in the darkness, it looked the same. An old truck was parked in front of it. He reached the edge of the property, pulled over to the side of the road and climbed out, shivering in the cold.

What am I doing? It's the middle of the night, and I can't get this place back.

He trudged through the snow to the fence, and his eyes adjusted to the night sky. An owl hooted somewhere nearby, and the sound comforted him, reminded him of the many nights he'd spent checking cattle over the years.

His heart lurched. He should have been living here, checking his own cattle, building a life he could be proud of. He curled his gloved hands around the top fence wire, staring into the night.

I was such a fool, trusting that jerk. I should have gotten a lawyer before I signed a thing.

Jerry's tale of owning and losing the sheep ranch came to mind. Clint didn't think less of him for losing his sheep operation. He understood. And Jerry had come out of it okay. He'd found a place at Rock Step. Started over with his wife by his side.

From far away he heard the low of a cow. He already missed Rock Step Ranch. Every day since he'd been hired there had been soul filling. He'd been content. Doing what made his soul sing.

How many times will I be punished, Lord? I'm sorry. I'm sorry for not waiting to buy this ranch. I wanted it so badly. If I'd waited a few years, I would have saved enough to get my own mortgage.

His chest burned within him, and his throat was tight as he tried to keep his emotions from erupting.

And, Lord, I'm sorry I lied to Lexi. She's right. I've been lying to myself.

It was time to face the truth. He was never meant to have it all—parents, a ranch, a wife and family. He didn't deserve it.

No one deserves it.

Where had that thought come from? He slid to his knees in the cold snow, the land he'd once owned spread out before him, and he prayed.

No one deserves it? I know I don't. But someone does. They must. Take Lexi, for example. She deserves it all.

The Bible verse he'd memorized came back. *For all have sinned and fall short of the glory of God.*

No one deserved anything but punishment.

Just as quickly, the rest of the verse came to mind. *All are justified freely by His grace through the redemption that came by Christ Jesus.*

The air whooshed out of his lungs.

Justified freely by His grace—undeserved, but given anyway.

You didn't just die for people who have their lives together. You know, the ones raised in loving homes and who are successful in life. You died for me. And I need a Savior more than anyone.

The cold air swirled around him, but he couldn't move. The memories he'd been avoiding—the best ones—all rushed back.

Lexi, so fearless and compassionate, showing him his cabin although she'd been wrecked with exhaustion. Riding out to the pasture with her and listening to her talk about her father. Making Thanksgiving dinner together, decorating his cabin for Christmas, all the Thursday meetings, kissing her under the imaginary mistletoe.

Priceless memories he'd cherish and revisit when his heart didn't throb with pain anymore.

No one but himself to blame. He'd brought this heartache on himself the same as he'd lost the land he knelt on.

Father, I've read the Bible enough to know I'm Your child. And You love me. So why can't I love myself? Is Lexi right? Do I push people away to make sure I'm alone? I don't want to be alone anymore.

He turned his head and caught his breath. A deer stood not ten feet away, chewing on prairie grass and watching him.

Clint laughed, big gulping guffaws, startling the deer. It leaped away.

God was always with him, and the deer was a reminder of it. Lurching to his feet, he brushed the snow off his knees and returned to the truck.

With God on his side, he could move forward. If he could just figure out a life without Lexi.

He'd left. And Lexi had never felt more alone.

She picked up the half-eaten muffins and threw them at the Christmas tree. A bulb fell to the floor and shattered. *Perfect.* She wanted to smash every ornament on the tree and drag it outside and let the wind blow it to Montana. Erase any sign of goodness and hope in this house.

This empty shell of a house.

She wiped her tears and took a deep breath.

Her parents were gone. Clint was gone. Her passion for Weddings by Alexandra was gone.

What was left?

A whine at the door startled her. She rushed to the door. Maybe Clint had come back. Maybe he hadn't meant what he'd said. Maybe…

She opened it, and Banjo slunk inside. No one else was around.

She choked, kneeling, and wrapped her arms around the dog. "He left you, too, didn't he? What are we going to do without him?"

Once more, she'd fallen for an emotionally unavailable guy. And it wasn't as if the warning signs hadn't been there all along. She'd told herself he was safe. Just a strong, silent cowboy. Someone she could depend on to manage the ranch and nothing more.

But she'd been wrong. He was more than a dependable ranch manager. He was caring, a great listener. He made time for her whenever she asked, and it wasn't because he was her employee. He cared about her needs. He made her feel safe and warm and loved.

But he didn't love her.

"Come on, Banjo." She padded to the living room. "Let's get you warm. Hop on the couch, and I'll get a blanket for us."

The poor dog tried to get up on the couch, but he couldn't. She heaved him up and he stretched out at one end.

She made her way to the hallway to find a blanket.

As much as she wanted to forget about Clint tonight, she couldn't. All the things she'd shared with him came to mind. Had her secrets meant nothing? Why wouldn't he have confided in her earlier? Surely he knew she wouldn't hold losing his property against him? Especially after being clued in to what his childhood had been like. His dedication to the smallest ranch details proved his integrity and intelligence.

He should have told her. Should have trusted her.

But what about before? Would I have still hired him if he'd told me during the interview? Yes, she still would have hired him. She believed in the best in people, and she'd needed a manager.

She opened the linen closet, but her favorite throw wasn't there. She'd forgotten she'd taken it to Denver.

The fact Clint had walked out was unforgivable. Didn't she have a say in whether he stayed or not? Had their kiss only been a silly game to him? Was she really just *sugar*, a moment of pretend and nothing more?

What had she thought would happen? That he would

suddenly become this grand gesture–making, romantic guy who bared his soul and wanted to spend his days with her?

Yes.

A tear slipped down her cheek, and then another.

What was she going to do now? She'd been ready to buy the building downtown, sell Natalie her company and live happily ever after here.

She'd already lost so much. To lose this dream of coming back, of starting a new business venture, was hard. But losing the hope she'd finally found the man to spend her life with—someone who shared her values, who loved the ranch like it was his own—she didn't think she'd recover from this. She just wanted to curl up with Banjo and sleep for days.

Daddy always kept a blanket on the top shelf of his closet. She went into his room and opened the closet door. The navy blanket was folded exactly where she knew it would be. She tried to reach it, but it was too high. She jumped, snagging it so that it fell to the floor. A shoe box crashed down, spilling its contents. Photographs, cards and other papers landed on the carpet.

She crouched, picking up the card closest to her. A birthday card she'd given him. The photo next to it had been taken last year. She and Daddy were grinning like fools with his arm slung over her shoulders and her arm wrapped around his waist. A swanky restaurant in Denver was the backdrop. She clutched it, remembering the way they'd laughed that night. A folded-up square caught her eye. She unfolded the glossy paper and gasped. It was the magazine article that launched Weddings by Alexandra into fame.

Every item she touched was related to her.

A keepsake box.

Full of a father's love.

Oh, Lord, I was wrong. How could I have been so wrong? I was angry at Daddy because I thought I had let him down, that he was mad at me.

Clint's parting words came back. *He probably didn't want to burden you.*

The words rang true. Daddy had loved her. And his death hadn't been a punishment. It had been his time. Nothing she could have done would have changed it. He was in one of those rooms in Heaven, and shouldn't she be happy for him? Living in paradise instead of suffering here?

She tucked everything back into the shoe box, took the blanket back to the living room and sat on the couch next to Banjo, spreading it over them.

Had she unintentionally burdened Clint with taking Daddy's place, not just in ranch operations, but as her friend and confidant? He'd helped her through a difficult time. His quiet understanding, the way he listened had helped her heal from her father's death.

Oh, God, I think from the day Clint walked in, I expected too much from him.

A sob erupted, and she started crying again. For her dead parents. For her own lonely future. For the company she no longer wanted. For the building she wouldn't be buying. But most of all for the man she loved who couldn't see himself as valuable. The one who'd left. The one she doubted she'd ever get over.

And when her eyes were swollen and no tears were left, she stared at the Christmas tree and felt as lost as the day she'd gotten the call Daddy had died.

Chapter Fourteen

"Let me make sure I have this correct." Nash Bolton held a piece of crispy bacon in his hand. Clint sat across the table from him in the kitchen of Wade's ranch house, where he'd driven after his meltdown last night. "Lexi Harrington not only hired you but has feelings for you, and you quit and drove here?"

"Yes." It sounded stupid, but how could Clint explain?

"And you say she's going to sell her successful business in Denver to move back to Wyoming."

"Uh-huh." He wasn't thirsty, but he took a drink of coffee anyway.

"And you told her, 'no, thank you,' yesterday because...? This is the part I'm confused about."

Clint pinched the bridge of his nose. "I told you. The ranch I lost? My fault. I signed a land contract with a man I didn't know, and I lost it all."

"Yeah, yeah, you explained that." Nash's eyes always seemed to hold mischief, and now was no exception. Clint wanted to wipe the smirk right off his face. He drank the rest of his coffee instead. "Listen, man, none of us had a real dad in our lives. Big Bob did his best for us at Yearling, but the way we all survived our childhoods, it's no wonder we had big dreams and no idea how to go about getting them. I did some stupid stuff, too, Clint. You can't beat yourself up over this."

Wade walked in and poured himself a cup of joe. "Looks like I'm missing the good stuff. What exactly are you beating yourself up for, Clint?"

Clint shifted his jaw, glaring at Nash. Nash sat back and opened his arms as if to say, *Tell him.* Clint might as well get it over with. No more secrets. Not from his friends. Not from anyone. He told Wade the basics, and when he'd finished, he ran his hand through his hair. What a morning.

"I've got a lawyer friend. One of the best in the state. She'll find this guy and get your money back."

Clint shook his head. "I talked to a lawyer after I was evicted. Devon skipped town after he stopped paying his loans, and apparently he was using a fake identity. There's nothing I can do. And, to be honest, I want to keep it in my past."

"Doesn't seem to be staying in the past," Nash muttered.

"What's that?" Wade asked.

"Well, it seems our boy Clint here has a thing going on with his boss."

"Lexi?" Wade leaned back, openly interested. "Do tell."

"Nash," Clint warned.

"Yes, she's been planning weddings and gotten quite successful at it in Denver, but it seems she's pretty set on moving back to Wyoming."

"What's this have to do with Clint?" Wade asked.

"Yeah, Clint," Nash said, acting innocent. "What does this have to do with you?"

Clint slammed his mug on the counter. "I'm in love with her." He spun to face them. "There. Are you happy?"

Their shocked expressions would have made him laugh on any other day.

"Does she love you?"

He shrugged. "If she does, it's based on a lie."

Nash raised his finger, leaning toward Wade. "Last night he told her about how he lost the land, and then he quit."

"You don't want a woman who is going to hold every mistake you make against you," Wade said. "Good riddance."

"She didn't hold it against me. *I* hold it against me."

"So you have reason to believe she cares for you, but you quit because of a mistake you made five years ago?"

"Yes." He pressed the heel of his hand into his eyebrow. "No. I don't know. She doesn't know me. Not the real me."

"Oh, ho!" Nash chuckled. "How many Clint Romines are there?"

"Nash," Wade scolded. "Clint, you're the quietest man I know. Always have been. You're kind of a mystery. But you're also the most loyal, honest, hardworking, humble man I know."

Wade thought that about him? Clint had to swallow the emotion building inside him.

"Hey, what about me?" Nash pretended to be hurt.

Wade ignored him and pointed at Clint. "There's only one you. You're genuine. The real deal."

"I want to believe it. As a kid I felt so worthless,

and—" Saying the word *worthless* choked him up. He shook his head, unable to continue.

"Me too." Nash's expression was sober, his eyes stone cold. "That's exactly the word I would use. *Worthless*."

Wade raised his eyebrows, took a sip of coffee and sighed. "I didn't just feel worthless. I *was* worthless."

Understanding knotted them together.

The mortar binding Clint's heart crumbled into dust.

"You were never worthless." Clint stared at Wade. Then he turned his attention to Nash. "And *you* were never worthless."

Nash squirmed in his chair.

"And I'm not worthless, either."

Wade crossed to Clint and pulled him into a side hug. Nash joined them and gave Clint a half embrace and a slap on the back before wiping under his eye with the back of his hand.

"You're my best friends," Clint said. "My brothers."

"You know it, brother." Nash pumped his fist in the air.

"So what are you going to do now?" Wade sat back down, and Nash and Clint followed.

He pictured Lexi, so anguished and angry last night, and he shook his head. "I don't know."

"You love her," Wade reiterated.

"Yep."

"She loves you?" Nash asked.

"I'm not sure."

"Well, tell us everything, and don't leave anything out." Nash crossed his arms over his chest.

What did he have to lose? He'd already turned his back on it all. "Well, it started in November…"

An hour later, they still sat around the table but in

complete silence. Clint had finished telling them everything.

"What makes you think you could have gotten better prices for the calves?" Wade asked. Clint should have figured he'd home in on the business stuff. Wade had built an empire complete with a working dude ranch, thousands of acres of land, a horse-breeding business and anything else that could make him money. The guy was a genius, and he'd done it all on his own. "That's the same price I got for mine."

Clint raised his eyebrows. He hadn't realized that.

"As far as the drunk kid, you couldn't have prevented it." Nash thumped his knuckles on the table. "Trust me. I know. My mother snuck around, stealing, drinking, drugging. No one could stop her. Still can't. I'm sure she's either in jail or smoking crack as we speak. You did the right thing, getting the cops involved."

"Sounds like you have some mighty thin excuses about why you can't be with Lexi." Wade sucked on a toothpick.

What had Lexi said last night? *Go cut yourself off from everyone. It's easier, isn't it? Then you don't have to take a chance and get your heart broken again.*

"I think you're right," Clint said. "I don't know love. I don't know how to do it. I'm scared of messing up."

Nash looked thoughtful. "What makes Lexi happy?"

That was easy. "Weddings. She loves planning them. And the building in Sweet Dreams—she's got all these ideas for it. She loves riding her horse, Nugget. And she gets all sparkly, like she's been dipped in glitter, when she's shopping for candles or jewelry. She loves decorating, and she misses her dad something fierce."

Wade and Nash exchanged shocked looks. "You need to go back. Tell her you love her."

"It's not enough."

"Sure, it is," Nash said.

"No, you don't understand. She deserves more."

"Then give it to her." Wade flourished his hand. "Buy the woman a ring. If you need money, I've got you covered."

"I've got money. Haven't spent more than two nickels since losing my land. It just piled up in the bank." In the past, Wade's offer would have embarrassed Clint, but today it made him grateful. "She's so generous. She makes other people's dreams come true for a living. She deserves to be swept off her feet. Dazzled."

Nash leaned forward. "How are you going to do it?"

"I'm going to need some help."

Lexi steeped a cup of tea and bent to pet Banjo, who looked up at her with what seemed to be hope. "I know you miss him. I do, too."

She'd finally drifted into a restless sleep around three in the morning and hadn't gotten out of bed until after noon. She'd yet to change out of her pajamas. What was the point?

Sitting cross-legged on the couch with the blanket nestled over her, she let the cup of tea warm her hands.

She needed a new life plan.

Did she still want to live on the ranch?

Maybe.

If she never saw Clint again, would she still want to live in Sweet Dreams and buy the building?

Maybe.

If she did see Clint again, would she want to live in Sweet Dreams?

She didn't know if her heart could handle bumping into him the way they'd left things, but if they made up…

Forget it. Not happening.

In any scenario, with Clint or without him, did she want to return to Denver and continue planning weddings there?

No.

Hmm…the suddenness of the no surprised her. Looked like she could cross one option off her list. She'd call Natalie later and fax her the proposal the lawyer had drawn up.

I want it all. I want to buy the building and renovate it into an elegant reception hall and plan weddings here. I want Clint back. I want him to manage the ranch with me as his wife.

Despair weighed on her.

She'd questioned Clint's feelings for her, but the past two months had said it all. Love was making a stranger soup when she was dead tired from grief over her father's death. Love was fixing her faucet and checking her fireplace to make sure she was safe. Love was driving her to church and playing pretend wedding at the building she'd asked him to inspect.

Love didn't have to be grand and sweeping.

Love had stared her in the face, taken care of her ranch, her employees, her horses and even her dog.

And what had she given him in return?

Maybe Clint couldn't see his value, but she did. The Bible passage she'd read the other day came to mind. *Do nothing out of selfish ambition or vain conceit.*

All her thoughts had been centering around her wants. What did Clint want? What did he need?

A ranch of his own.

An idea hit her so suddenly, she almost gasped.

Lord, I don't know. This is extreme. Even for me.

When she thought of all she'd been given over the years, though—parents who loved her, this loving home, not one worry about money—the idea didn't seem so extreme.

Maybe she was always meant to be the maker of grand gestures. No one deserved one more than Clint.

And she was going to give him one. No strings attached.

Really, Lord? I want to do Your will. Not my own.

Pulling up the Bible app on her phone, she typed in Philippians chapter two and read the entire thing. Then she came back to the fourth verse. *Rather, in humility value others above yourselves, not looking to your own interests but each of you to the interests of others.* She jumped up and ran to her bedroom. Threw on jeans and a sweater. Then she hurried downstairs, pulled on a coat and jogged to the ranch office.

"Jerry?" She stopped short in the doorway, trying to catch her breath.

"Miss Lexi? Get in here. You look as spooked as the horses before a lightning storm. What happened?"

"I need some advice."

His wide-eyed expression held fear. "I don't know. I'm not the best person for that."

"Clint left. He told me he was putting in his two weeks and he left."

"I was wonderin' where he went off to. Logan said his truck was gone."

"I want him back."

"Well, I reckon we all want him back. Why'd he quit? Those goings-on the other night?"

"I love him."

Jerry just about fell off his stool.

"I scared him away, Jerry. And he had a terrible childhood, got swindled out of the only thing he ever wanted, and he has all this misplaced guilt about catching Jake drinking on the job."

"Well, seems there's a lot of suds in the bucket, missy." Jerry rubbed his chin. "What makes you think you scared him off?"

"I… Well…" She hunched over like a truant schoolgirl. "I'm me. I'm too intense, and I pushed him into feelings he probably didn't want, and—"

"He might not have wanted those feelings, but he had them, and it wasn't due to you pushing or whatnot. He loves you. It was as clear as the signs a cow's about to give birth."

She grimaced. Love was similar to a cow going into labor? *Ew.* She shook her head. "I ruined it. I got pretty mad, and I yelled some things, and, well, I told him to get out."

"Before or after he quit?" He appeared deep in thought.

"After. Why?"

"Okay. I think we can work with that. Yes, sirree, I think we can."

Work with what?

"See here, Clint's like the moose. He's a loner, but strong, and sometimes moose—"

"Jerry, I'm sorry, but I don't have the brains to figure out the moose analogy today." She took a seat on the stool next to him. "Without Clint, what happens to this ranch?"

He frowned, shaking his head. "I don't know, sweetheart. You'll have to hire someone else, I guess."

"What if I didn't? I got this crazy idea, and I need to know your opinion."

"Shoot."

She explained it as best she could, and for the next twenty minutes she and Jerry volleyed questions and answers back and forth. Then Jerry grinned.

"If you go through with this and that boy doesn't get on his knees and beg you to marry him, I'll kick him straight in the keister, and you can count on that."

"I'm not doing this to get a proposal, Jerry." She hopped off the stool to leave. "I'm doing this because it's right. For Clint. For the ranch. Do you think Daddy would have approved?"

"Yes. I do. He'd want to see the ranch taken care of, and he'd want you to be protected financially. You're a smart 'un, Miss Lexi."

She hugged him tightly. "Thanks, Jerry. I don't know what I'd do without you."

Chapter Fifteen

Christmas Eve morning arrived with a fresh fall of snow and gentle flakes floating in the air. Clint opened the sliding door to the old shed.

"Thanks for helping me, Jerry." Clint clapped him on the shoulder. "We'll have to move out the old hay wagon first."

"Just glad to have you back." His big grin looked like it held a secret. "Miss Lexi is going to like this."

"Well, I'm glad you think so. I've got some apologies to make. I hope she'll hear me out."

"Something tells me she'll be all ears." They moved inside. "She's like a filly. High-strung with a heart of gold. Spirit. And class..."

Clint tuned out the filly talk and dragged the tarp off the sleigh. All day yesterday he and Wade and Nash had planned, shopped and prepped for this. The first hurdle had been driving into Rock Step Ranch undetected this morning. Since he'd arrived at 5:00 a.m., he'd made it without seeing Lexi. He'd called Jerry last night and asked for his help this morning. Thankfully, the man agreed without giving Clint a lecture.

"I'll be right back. Charger can pull these out faster than we can." Jerry pivoted to leave. "In the meantime, you get the sleigh cleaned up. The missus sent some blankets for the ride."

"Okay." As Clint polished the sleigh, he reviewed the plan. He needed to shower and get dressed. The flowers were in his fridge. And the other item was safely tucked away in the cabin. His heartbeat had been tapping out Morse code distress signals for hours, but he figured that was his body resisting the threat of laying his soul bare.

He *would* lay his soul bare.

Soon.

It didn't take long to get the sleigh cleaned up. He ran back to his cabin, his nerves still jittery. After showering, he was buttoning his dress shirt when he heard a knock on the door.

He answered it and stopped breathing. Lexi stood before him with her hair in waves down her shoulders. She wore a black jacket, revealing a red dress that hugged her body. Black heels made her seem taller, more sophisticated than he was used to, and her makeup accented her eyes.

"You're beautiful."

She blinked. "Thank you. Jerry told me you were here. Can I come in?"

She looked nervous, and the way she briefly touched her ear before nodding made him want to reassure her. "Let's go to the living room." He took her jacket and draped it over the back of a chair.

Banjo followed her inside, sat at Clint's feet and let out a yowl.

"I missed you, too, buddy." He patted his head.

Lexi handed him a slim folder. A slither of unease went down his spine. What was this?

"Go ahead. Open it."

Warily, he obliged. He drew his eyebrows together as he realized it was a partnership agreement. His head swam. This couldn't be what he thought it was. He'd read it wrong, or she'd been fooled by an attorney. It didn't make sense.

"No way." He snapped the folder shut, handing it back to her. How could she even think to give up her inheritance? After all he'd confessed…

"I want you to run this ranch, but not as my employee, as part owner. I'll be a silent partner. Rock Step Ranch will be yours to run, to manage, to live on. I'll take a portion of the profit. You would never have to see me." Her brown eyes pleaded with him to understand, but he didn't. He only knew one thing. The woman standing before him was better than anyone he'd ever met. He loved her with an intensity he'd never thought possible.

"I don't want this ranch," he said. "I can't believe you'd even think to do this. This is your inheritance, your home. It belongs to you. I could never let you give it away."

Her eyes filled with tears. He was messing this up. It wasn't what he'd planned. He'd never imagined she would show up and blow him away with this incredible offer.

"I'm sorry, Lexi. The other night—you were right. About everything." Her perfume drifted to him, and it was all he could do not to crush her to him. "I did push you away, and I was stuck in my past. I never thought someone like you would look twice at me. And from the moment you hired me, I was attracted to you. I knew it wasn't smart, but I couldn't help being drawn to you."

"I didn't help with that." She looked at the floor. "I was so lonely. I pushed you into spending time with me."

"You didn't have to push hard. Those times we spent together are precious to me. No matter what happens, I will hold onto them forever."

"What do you think is going to happen?" She wrapped her arms around her waist.

"I don't know. But I know this. I love you. I think it's the coolest thing that you plan weddings for a living. You bless so many people. I feel like you live to make people's dreams come true. When you decorated my cabin for Christmas—I was blown away. You're smart and kind and honest and true. I'm not the romantic guy you deserve, but I want to be your tiger. Do you know what I'm saying?"

Lexi couldn't stop her lips from wobbling. Clint looked like he'd stepped out of a men's magazine. She couldn't stop staring. At first she thought he was turning down her offer because he was set on leaving, but… had he just said he loved her? "I know what you're saying. I'm sorry, too, Clint. I pushed you. Expected you to be everything here—the manager, my confidant, even my handyman—"

"I wanted to be all those things."

"But I never thought about how it affected you."

"It affected me in the best way it could. You showed me what love looks like. Your friendship—you gave it to me freely without questions or strings."

"I needed you." Tears threatened again.

"I've never been needed. Not by anyone. Do you know how great it is to be needed?" He gently clasped her arms. "I'd been trapped in nothingness for years, and working here, meeting you, spending time with you was like breathing fresh air after being locked in prison. Thank you."

"I still need you." She touched his cheek.

His eyes darkened. "You do?"

"Yes. I love you, too, Clint." She blinked. "But I don't want to trap you. You gave me my life back, my smile, my joy. You helped me make peace with Daddy's death. And you never asked for anything in return."

"You'd already given me the world."

"I love you, Clint, and that's why I had these papers drawn up. You deserve your own ranch."

"I don't want any ranch unless you come with it." He hurried to the kitchen, grabbed the roses and came back, handing them to her. "This wasn't how I planned it, but these are for you."

"Blush colored." She inhaled their scent. "My favorite. How did you know?"

"Well, the silky squares in your office are all pink." Clint took her hand in his and dropped to one knee. "Alexandra Harrington, I love you. I don't deserve you, will never deserve you, but I'll do my best to make you happy every day of your life. Will you do me the honor of marrying me?"

He reached into his pocket, took out a square jeweler's box and opened it. The diamond engagement ring she'd swooned over in Sweet Dreams Jewelers winked at her. She covered her mouth with her hand, shaking her head in wonder. "How did you know? It's the exact one I picked out, but I never told anyone."

"I saw it and knew. It was you." He still looked up at her. "Well?"

"Yes!" She drew him to his feet. "A million times, yes!"

He tenderly slipped the ring on her finger and tugged her into his arms. Then he bent his head and claimed her lips. Her knees wobbled as she sank into his kiss.

When he broke away, he smiled, pressing his forehead to hers. Her cell phone rang. Lexi checked it and grinned. She had to take this call.

"I'm at your house with the puppy," Dan Smith said. "Should I come back later?"

"No. Drive to the cabins. I'll meet you out front." She ended the call and spun to face Clint. "I have a surprise for you, too. Come on." She opened the door and stood on his porch.

He followed, a questioning look on his face.

Dan parked his truck and approached them with a border collie puppy in his hands. "Hope I didn't come too early. Lola's got a ham in the oven, and she'll have my head if I don't deliver this before our guests arrive for supper."

"Thank you so much, Dan. Please tell Lola merry Christmas for me."

"Will do. Merry Christmas, Lexi. Sure is nice to have you back."

Lexi held the wiggly black-and-white fluff ball and turned, almost crashing into Clint.

"This is for you, tiger." She grinned, holding the puppy out to him. "Your first puppy. All yours. Merry Christmas."

To her surprise, his eyes welled up. He took the dog in his arms and cradled it. "I can't believe you got me a dog. My own dog. No one has ever gotten me a gift like this."

"You needed a dog."

"I don't know what to say. Thank you." He drew her

into his embrace, the puppy between them, and kissed her. "I love you, sugar."

"I couldn't love you more, tiger."

He looked like he was going to kiss her again, but he checked his watch. "Wait here. Get your jacket on. I'll be back in a few minutes." He handed her the dog, yanked a coat out of the closet and ran up the drive.

What was that all about? Not knowing what to think, she set the puppy down. He and Banjo sniffed each other as she eased into her jacket. The sound of bells reached her ears, and she peeked out the window.

Clint drove the horse-drawn sleigh. She scooped up the puppy and raced outside. He stopped the horses, jumped down and kissed her. Thoroughly.

"Your ride, my lady." He gestured to the sleigh.

"Oh, Clint, I used to love riding around with Daddy and Mama."

"You don't mind riding around with me? I don't want you to be sad." He helped her onto the bench next to him and covered her, Banjo and the puppy with blankets.

"I want nothing more than to ride around with you." She stared into his eyes. "Thank you, Clint."

He grinned. "That's tiger to you."

She laughed. "Well, the tiger I know would have some mistletoe ready for this moment."

Clint lifted a sprig of mistletoe above her head.

"Way ahead of you, sugar."

Epilogue

He'd been engaged just shy of a year, but married life beckoned. Clint reached for Lexi's hand, squeezed it and reached for the handle of the church door.

"We're married." His gaze swept from the white veil and tiara on top of her shiny dark hair down her beautiful wedding gown until stopping at their joined hands, two rings sparkling on their fingers.

"We are. We're finally married." She looked up at him with a massive smile. He opened the door and helped her down the church steps.

Fat snowflakes drifted to the ground, and at the end of the sidewalk, Coco and Charger stamped their feet, waiting to pull the sleigh with the Just Married sign attached to the back. Wedding guests congratulated them as they hurried down the sidewalk.

He helped her up, still in shock that she was actually his. Jerry had done the honors of escorting her down the aisle. *Thank You, Lord. I lost a run-down piece of property, but I gained a wife and the best ranch in Wyoming. My wildest dreams couldn't have come up with this.*

Clint drove the sleigh past snow-covered pines on the country lane that led into town.

"When we get back from our honeymoon," Lexi said, settling under the blankets, "we'll have to call the ranch in Idaho and tell them we have the hay they need for their horses."

"No ranch business today, Mrs. Romine." He grinned at her. "We agreed."

"But Daddy's dream—we did it." She hooked her arm under his and leaned against his shoulder.

"He'd be proud of you." Clint smiled at her. "For the ranch and for moving your business here."

Lexi had bought the building downtown earlier this year. She insisted on keeping the name of the building the Department Store, but she had a Weddings by Alexandra sign made for the door. Their wedding reception would be the debut of the Department Store's new role as the go-to reception hall in Sweet Dreams. Together, he and Lexi had hired contractors and planned the space. All the construction and refinishing had been worth it.

The horses turned onto the side street, thankfully still snow-covered, that led to the reception.

"Are you ready to christen your building?" he asked.

"I am. Let's go!"

As soon as they arrived, Clint jumped down from the sleigh and carried Lexi into the building to a round of applause. He placed her back on her feet and whispered, "Don't be long, sugar."

She flashed him a grin and winked. Amy hustled Lexi up the stairs and out of sight. Clint couldn't stop watching her the entire time.

People were milling around on the main floor, soft music filled the air, and his best friends Wade and Marshall clapped him on the back. The only one missing was Nash, who had called Clint two days ago sounding devastated, explaining he had an emergency and couldn't come to the wedding.

"I couldn't be happier for you, tiger." Dottie dabbed her eyes and gave him a long hug.

"Let the boy up for air." Big Bob pulled her back then shook Clint's hand. "Congratulations, son."

"Ladies and gentlemen, direct your attention to the stairs." Wade held the microphone.

Clint took his spot—the same spot he'd stood in almost a year ago—and held his breath as Lexi descended. She'd never been prettier, and the mischievous smile on her face told him she was remembering their moment, too. She lifted her skirt as she came down, her other hand trailing the railing.

When she reached the second step from the bottom, Clint swung her off her feet, twirling her until she stood before him. Everyone cheered.

"You mesmerize me, sugar."

"You're pretty easy on the eyes yourself, tiger." She wound her arms around his neck. "What are you going to do now?"

"Well, there is mistletoe."

She looked up. A branch of mistletoe hung from the ceiling.

"You're pretty sly, tiger," she whispered. "Why don't you show me what you've got?"

He didn't need to be asked twice. He kissed her, the first in a lifetime of mistletoe kisses.

"Anything for you, sugar."

* * * * *

If you enjoyed this story,
pick up these other books by Jill Kemerer:

SMALL-TOWN BACHELOR
UNEXPECTED FAMILY
HER SMALL-TOWN ROMANCE
YULETIDE REDEMPTION
HOMETOWN HERO'S REDEMPTION

Available now from Love Inspired!

Dear Reader,

I hope you enjoyed the first book in the Wyoming Cowboys series. I had so much fun researching ranches and Wyoming that I wish I could visit the fictional town of Sweet Dreams. Clint and Lexi are dear to me. Clint had been neglected and abused throughout his life, and it was no wonder he held himself to impossible standards. Raised in a home rich in love, Lexi found herself vulnerable and questioning her future at the prospect of being all alone in life. I loved watching these two bring out the best in each other even as they fought their insecurities and learned to trust God with their future.

Clint's best friends and foster brothers, Nash, Marshall and Wade, will be thrust on their own romantic journeys in the rest of the series. But love and trust doesn't come easily for any of them. This Christmas, I pray that your past hurts are healed and that you spend time capturing the glorious reason for the season. You can be certain you have a Father who loves you, a Savior who lived, died and rose for you, and a Spirit who guides you. This love can't be earned. It's freely given. To you. To me. Merry Christmas!

Blessings to you,
Jill Kemerer

COMING NEXT MONTH FROM
Love Inspired®

Available October 17, 2017

SECRET CHRISTMAS TWINS
Christmas Twins • by Lee Tobin McClain

Erica Lindholm never expected her Christmas gift would be becoming guardian to twin babies! But fulfilling her promise to keep their parentage a secret becomes increasingly difficult when her holiday plans mean spending time with—and falling for—their uncle, Jason Stephanidis, on the family farm.

AN AMISH PROPOSAL
Amish Hearts • by Jo Ann Brown

Pregnant and without options, Katie Kay Lapp is grateful when past love Micah Stoltzfus helps her find a place to stay. But when he proposes a marriage of convenience, she refuses. Because Katie Kay wants much more—she wants the heart of the man she once let go.

CHRISTMAS ON THE RANCH
by Arlene James and Lois Richer

Spend Christmas with two handsome ranchers in these two brand-new holiday novellas, where a stranger's joyful spirit provides healing for one bachelor, and a single mom with a scarred past is charmed by her little girl's wish for a cowboy daddy.

THE COWBOY'S FAMILY CHRISTMAS
Cowboys of Cedar Ridge • by Carolyne Aarsen

Returning to the Bar W Ranch, Reuben Walsh finds his late brother's widow, Leanne, fighting to keep the place running. Reuben's committed to helping out while he's around—even if it means spending time with the woman who once broke his heart. Can they come to an agreement—and find a happily-ever-after in time for the holidays?

THE LAWMAN'S YULETIDE BABY
Grace Haven • by Ruth Logan Herne

Having a baby dropped on his doorstep changes everything for state trooper Gabe Cutter. After asking widowed single mom next door Corinne Gallagher for help, he's suddenly surrounded by the lights, music and holiday festivities he's avoided for years. This Christmas, can they put their troubled pasts behind and create a family together?

A TEXAS HOLIDAY REUNION
Texas Cowboys • by Shannon Taylor Vannatter

After his father volunteers Colson Kincaid to help at Resa McCall's ranch over Christmas, the single dad is reunited with his old love. Colson's used to managing horses, but can he keep his feelings for Resa from spilling over—and from revealing a truth about his daughter's parentage that could devastate them forever?

LOOK FOR THESE AND OTHER LOVE INSPIRED BOOKS WHEREVER BOOKS ARE SOLD, INCLUDING MOST BOOKSTORES, SUPERMARKETS, DISCOUNT STORES AND DRUGSTORES.

LICNM1017